Shadowed Skies

For Esmé, may your wings carry you through life's uncharted skies with resilience and courage.

Shadowed Skies

by Haley Cavanagh

OUR STREET
BOOKS

London, UK
Washington, DC, USA

CollectiveInk

First published by Our Street Books, 2025
Our Street Books is an imprint of Collective Ink Ltd.,
Unit 11, Shepperton House, 89 Shepperton Road, London, N1 3DF
office@collectiveinkbooks.com
www.collectiveinkbooks.com
www.Ourstreet-Books.com

For distributor details and how to order please visit the 'Ordering' section on our website.

Text copyright: Haley Cavanagh 2024

ISBN: 978 1 80341 771 4
978 1 80341 772 1 (ebook)
Library of Congress Control Number: 2024930547

A CIP catalogue record for this book is available from the British Library.

Design: Lapiz Digital Services

UK: Printed and bound by CPI Group (UK) Ltd, Croydon, CR0 4YY
Printed in North America by CPI GPS partners

We operate a distinctive and ethical publishing philosophy in all areas of our business, from our global network of authors to production and worldwide distribution.

Acknowledgments

I would like to extend my heartfelt thanks to Collective Ink Books for their unwavering support and belief in this project. A special thanks to the dedicated editorial team whose insights and expertise have shaped this book into its final form.

My deepest appreciation goes to my husband and lifelong companion, Luke, whose artistic brilliance brought the cover to life. Your talent and support mean the world to me.

To everyone who has supported and believed in me, your encouragement fuels my belief in myself. Your presence is a constant reminder that anything is possible with a strong support system.

A nod to the unconventional beginnings of this journey— initially dictating this book in the carpool lane at my children's school during NaNoWriMo 2019. If I can craft a novel amidst the chaos, anyone can surely conquer the extraordinary.

As we navigate the skies of life, may each of you be granted wings to soar above challenges and embrace the boundless possibilities that await.

With immense gratitude,
Haley Cavanagh

Other Works by This Author:

Astraeus, ISBN: 1948185601
Retaliation, ISBN: 1675666342
Adulting: The Ultimate Cheat Sheet

Chapter One

River

I take a deep breath, struggling in vain as the burly soldier drags me through the imposing steel gates. His ironclad grip digs into my arm, certain to leave bruises. Panic and desperation rise within me.

The Compound, a sprawling underground bunker beneath the city, is where they imprison us Evol-humans. In the sterile labs, scientists conduct painful experiments and harvest our organs without remorse. The white halls filled with doctors, soldiers, glass specimen tubes, and cold machinery create a high-tech nightmare for my kind.

My people never asked to be created—the product of military experiments splicing avian DNA into humans to create a new breed of super-soldiers. But the experiments went too far, and now my winged kind are hunted and imprisoned.

With each hurried step beneath the stark floodlights, the shadows around the Compound seem to reach for me with claw-like fingers. I can't let this soldier take me to the lab where many others have faced endless torment. They took my twin brother Porter a month ago, trapping him in a net during a supply run. I tried freeing him, but drones hauled him away before I could cut him loose.

With a violent wrench, I finally break free of the soldier's viselike grip. My wings slice the air as gunfire whistles past me. I drive higher, escaping into the inky night sky above the Compound's walls.

Jagged mountain peaks loom ahead. Beyond them, freedom awaits—if I can make it.

I collapse onto the snow-blanketed plateau, sharp rocks biting into my raw, tender hands. Pine trees rustle all around me, carrying the crisp scent of cedar. I slump against the cold stone, my chest heaving as I try to steady my pounding heart. I'm free at last. The shouts of my pursuers fade on the wind.

As I scan my new mountain sanctuary, the vast emptiness strikes me.

"Hello?" My voice cracks, echoing in the stillness. Only the wind's eerie moan responds.

I'm alone.

But not for long.

Three months later

The half-clouded Utah sky hints at a coming storm—perfect hunting weather. In the predawn dusk, I scan the blighted valley through my binoculars. No signs of life remain in this post-apocalyptic wasteland, just abandoned buildings and ghost towns.

Good. I can hunt in peace.

My hidden camp atop the canyon is the ideal vantage point. Tracking devices falter up here, and communications fizzle out. The biting chill braces me as I plunge into the forest below, exhilarated by flight. These mountains never get old. Here, I'm invincible.

Perched on an aspen branch, I scan for prey, securing my tattered burlap sack. It's threadbare but easy to grab food on the go. Last week, I hit the jackpot with apples from a lone fruit tree. They've become scarce over the previous two decades in the aftermath of the Scourge.

But today's my lucky day because a buck emerges from a hidden thicket. I don't waste time.

With a choked whimper, the buck collapses, my arrow lodged in its heart.

I lower my bow and approach with quiet footsteps, murmuring "Thank you" under my breath. I always honor the sacrifice of the creatures that sustain me. Kneeling beside the fresh kill, I unsheathe my knife and slice its belly to begin field dressing. Years of practice guide my hands as I remove the entrails, wasting none of the precious meat. Blood steams the chill autumn air as I work, the rich iron scent mingling with damp earth and pine.

The work is methodical, almost soothing. Slice, separate, and discard. My hands know this ritual, allowing my mind to wander. Winter's icy teeth will soon be at my doorstep. I need to redouble my efforts in preserving meat while the hunting is good. I lash the buck's hind legs to a sturdy branch and haul the kill over my shoulders. The trek back to my nest will be long, and flying there with the extra weight sucks, but it will give the meat time to cool and firm.

When I crest the ridge overlooking my hidden valley, the afternoon sun dips below the mountains, casting the forest in deep, dusky blues. A few months ago, the canyons were a vibrant canvas of gold, oranges, and reds. I spent most of my time chewing scenery, hiding, and hunting game. I scan for signs of intrusion out of habit, then glide to my plateau sanctuary. Pine boughs and brush conceal my modest camp, with only a thin trail of smoke giving me away.

I lay the buck down, stretching my aching shoulders to catch the cool breeze. Every rustle in the bushes, every pattern crossing the sky, makes me tuck my wings in closer. Their sheer size makes hiding a challenge.

I push aside the memories—*time to prepare*. I drink thirstily from the rainwater barrel, then wash the blood from my hands and forearms. Night falls fast in these parts. Soon, frost will creep across the stones. I prep a fire lay with flint and kindling at the ready. I've got to cook and preserve this ahead of sunset.

Sleet needles my cheeks as I bend to turn a wild kill into life-giving nourishment.

I'm all that's left of my kind. To others, we're freaks—abominations.

It wasn't always this way. They've hunted us for decades—from when those secret human experiments fused our DNA with avian genes meant to create resilient astronauts. Instead, we colonized Earth.

I'm part of the second Evol-human generation, born to cadets with wings. Our evolution accelerated, manifesting abnormalities like webbed feet or gills. A rare few, Pops said, could read minds. Never met one, but it's possible.

I'm River Shaw—eighteen, alone, and hunted.

But still breathing.

Chapter Two

Delene

The icy metal bars chill my fingers. This sterile prison reeks of harsh cleaning products, barely masking the underlying sickness that permeates the Stockade.

I'm in one of many cages lining the walls of this underground bunker the humans use for imprisoning my kind. Because of our creation through experimental evolution—a splice of human, avian, and reptilian genes that makes us stronger and able to breathe at high altitudes—they call us "Evol-humans." They keep us caged like animals, harvesting our blood.

The florescent lights overhead cast everything in an eerie, sterile glow. I avoid touching anything, not wanting to relive the problematic memories imprinted on this cruel place. My mother had what she called "the touch"—psychic impressions left on objects by those who handled them before. She passed some of that sensitivity to my sister Lily and me. Once, holding the cell bars too long, I felt the prisoners' despair for days. I never want to relive that.

So I withdraw into myself, determined not to let them break me. I won't give them the satisfaction. Someday, I'll escape this nightmare.

They claimed my sister died of disease during interrogation, but I felt her pain. Her anguish and loss gutted me. They destroyed Lily, the best sister imaginable.

Ironically, they feared the unknown yet created us, blind to the consequences. When threatened, humans seek to destroy their opposition. Unfortunately for us, we're it.

Lily, ever radiant, was Mom's "Sunbeam." On the other hand, I stick out like a sore thumb and always have done so.

My mom said I have no filter, which is true. I say whatever's on my mind. There's no point in walking on eggshells, not in this world. Without honesty, I'm nothing.

No matter how they torment me, I've refused to eat or utter a word for days.

I've been captive here for months. They keep me locked and tortured in this cage. But I won't let them break me. I'm on a hunger strike, yet they still tamper with my food schedule. They often starve me if I don't give them what they want. I don't know how long I've been here, but I will get out or die trying.

From my cage's corner, his whistling reaches me before the citrusy waft of his aftershave. I grit my teeth. *Ugh, the syrupy song he always whistles.* His voice is so cheerful, with a little vibrato twist. I stare at the floor.

His whistling halts. He clicks his expensive shoes together like a soldier at attention. He's older than my dad would be, attractive for his age. He meticulously styles his full head of silver hair with the attentive vanity of a much younger man. His wolfish grin unsettles me, friendly yet sinister.

"Good morning, little angel," he chirps, his singsong voice almost painfully cheerful, like the first day of summer vacation.

As far back as I can go, I glare daggers at him beneath the curtain of my hair. Oblivious, Dr. Lytle saunters toward me, whistling a jaunty tune as he flips through his clipboard.

"Delene Fairborne, Delene *Fairborne.* Seventeen years old, blood type O-positive, currently non-negotiable and *refusing* to cooperate." He knows this, but he knocks his pen against the clipboard, tap-dancing the length across the paper as if he's got better things to do. He hums. "Says here you haven't eaten in two days. That'll kick anyone in the teeth. You've got to be hungry, right?" He peers through the bars, and his pale eyes bore into me like ice picks.

I focus on the elegant script on his doctor's coat: *Dr. Martin Lytle, M.D.*

"We don't want to starve you, kiddo. Why not comply, take the tests, and eat?" He steps forward when I don't respond and curls his hand around a bar.

Closer, I think. *Come closer.*

"You're not still upset with me about Lily, are you? She developed an infection. We did our best."

"You're the real plague here, Doc," I challenge through gritted teeth.

He frowns, his thick eyebrows lowered. "What? I missed that."

I move on all fours toward the bars. My long wings graze the bars to either side. I fold them inward and move in for the kill. Fear flickers across his features, but he doesn't move. He struggles to keep his mask of indifference, and we're locked in a battle of futility. I clasp my hands around his on the bars as he senses what I'm about to do.

He jerks violently. I'd done this once and discovered he knew my grandfather. He spearheaded the experiment resulting in Evol-humans and has done since our inception.

Dr. Lytle's past flashes before my eyes, and I sense his dread. I try not to pry too far into people's thoughts and trauma, but this time, I go straight to where it hurts. Without the mercy I usually reserve for those I care for, I hiss, "You left your men behind. You deserted them, Martin, and left them for dead in Iraq. Your superiors believed your lies, and they rewarded you. They *decorated* you for being a killer."

He pales as the ghosts of the past travel through us—the stench of gunfire and blood haunts his heart. I stand as high as the cage allows and gaze at him. He shudders, pale, but I don't let go. "You're afraid. You are afraid at night when they come to haunt you. Gonzales, Fischer, Callahan, your whole unit. You act with cruelty, but the truth is, deep inside, you're nothing but a scared little boy. A cowardly, selfish, scared—" I hiss. "The military shattered your humanity long ago. Now you pretend your cruelty serves some higher cause, but it's all a lie to bury your weakness."

He rips away. *"Enough."* He wipes his forearm across his forehead. He stares, disbelieving, as I clutch the bars and pant. Righteous anger fills me for what they did to Lily. "All right," he breathes. "Have it your way. Do you want to starve? You'll starve." He leans closer. "And then, I'll harvest your Evol-human organs for scrap and keep your pretty, snowbell white wings as a souvenir, as I did with your *sister*."

I won't give him the satisfaction of my shock. I expected this. I glare until he walks away, then I return to my corner.

Our kind has been called many things over the years—all names for the same scientifically created race. Those first secret trials gave us hollow, lightweight bones and heightened lung capacity. Our alular digit helps steer our flight.

The goal was to create enhanced people to colonize harsh extraterrestrial environments. But the wartime chemical weapons outbreak known as the Scourge soon following our creation decimated most of the planet's population. We "Evol-humans" happened to be immune, making us both pariahs and saviors to the survivors desperate for our blood.

My grandfather said he fled with his pregnant wife after the military trials combining human, avian, and reptilian DNA. My mother was born nine months later in a dusty, abandoned attic, a sweet baby with wings. Decades later, she met my father when she flew to a mall rooftop as they scavenged.

He was like her, aerial and alone. They fell in love, and he joined my family. They stayed under the radar for years as they kept on the move and scraped by for survival. The radio frequencies broadcasted the call for blood donations, and word about the super city in the valley spread. They built the city in Utah, the one place not decimated, the agriculture still alive due to the high elevation. The mountains were still intact, and the air was fresh. They lied to lure our kind with promises of a haven free from bloodshed.

My mom always said my grandpa was wise. When they killed him one day, we took refuge in a bunker he had built. Lily and I were born inside it. He handcrafted the bunker at his farm in Colorado long before they recruited him for testing, and thankfully, the farm was so well-hidden that no one found us. But all good things come to an end, and eventually, on the heel of a few safe years, the food ran out.

When we emerged into the world, I was six, Lily was eight, and the farmland around us had become rubble.

As we migrated from place to place in our beat-up pickup truck, my parents kept tabs on the news through our staticky radio, translating the propaganda. We'd scan the empty highways, scavenging goods from ghost towns and abandoned military depots. At night, we'd take inventory of our gasoline, ammunition, and food supplies, making plans to ration sparingly. During the day, my parents trained us to fight, fly, and survive.

Occasionally, we came upon another of our kind. Still, once my parents heard about the slaughter and harvesting, they decided it was better to keep to ourselves.

They stayed far away from the city, but the bombs destroyed the forestry and farmland, and there was nowhere else to go.

We can breathe at high altitudes, heal rapidly, and fly. The second generation evolved humanity at an accelerated rate.

We were the result of their many phases. They've called us lots of different things, "Fae" for the whimsical mystics, "Freaks" for the fearful, "Winged Ones" for the romantics, and my personal favorite, "Scum of the Earth" for the self-deluded elitists. The debate about the ethics of our existence doesn't change anything. They were committed to destroying each other, and they succeeded. They wiped out themselves in the process. Great job, Earth.

My mom described those times as the early days when survivors banded together, and people shunned us. After building the city and the survivors coming together, they pursued us for our blood and unique rapid-healing ability. Dad always said they meant to germinate half-human, half-Evol hybrid embryos, but their plans never worked out.

Years later, the viral Scourge pandemic wiped out over 75 percent of the population. The surviving humans picked themselves apart with wars over resources. Finally, they scraped together what was left and built the supercity. They weren't aware our blood was the answer then. When the dust settled and survivors banded together, a disease struck. They called this one the Atom Plague.

Unlike anything they'd ever witnessed, a person's skin would wilt without symptoms or warning, reducing them to ash.

My grandparents often told me about life inside the city walls. They watched the human population diminish daily as the Atom Plague took its toll. The medical technology of their time was woefully inadequate, and they would recount stories of doctors, helpless against the mysterious illness causing raging fevers, searing nerve pain, and failure of vital organs. They spoke of funeral pyres that smoldered day and night.

With humanity's preservation at stake, scientists scrambled for answers. They found iron concentrations in humans implode when infected with the plague, killing them.

Evol-human blood can reverse the plague's effects and immunize vulnerable people. But they ran into trouble with blood donor shortages. Humans became desperate to survive by any means necessary. At first, those wealthy enough who had the means procured a spot in line. As time went on and desperation reigned, they hunted us. My mom once said a man kept a whole family in his basement for years, harvesting their blood to keep himself alive. They were frantic to get their hands on us.

People came from miles around, desperate for a haven in the city. But soon, the city became too crowded, and they didn't let everyone in. The steel walls rose, and our kind fled to the mountains for safety.

In their desperation, they scattered flyers over the canyons. They promised asylum to those who willingly donated blood.

The first wave of Evol-humans, deceived by lies, perished immediately. The rest went into hiding, eventually picked off by Dr. Lytle's enforcers.

We never stayed in the same place, except one winter, when my father found a cabin hidden deep in the forest, covered in vines. For a few cold months, the cabin became our home.

In captivity, I've clung to a particular memory for strength.

I'm younger, and I sit cross-legged on a worn-out carpet. Sunshine pours like wine through the broken patch of the attic roof, illuminating the dust mites around us. I'm in the center of an essential donut of forgotten and deteriorated toys—a battered doll, an old, rusty pocket watch, a worn and faded baseball glove, and a teacup with a chipped lip.

Lily leans against the attic door a few feet away, rolling her lips in as she worries. "Are you sure you want to do this, Dee?" Lily asks.

I gather a lungful of air. "Yes. I must understand and control it, or I'll be out of control."

Lily's eyes slide to the teacup. She leans in, her expression earnest. "Maybe that one first. It belonged to Grandma. Something of hers might be the safest, like stepping into shallow waters."

My fingertip grazes the chipped crack. Grandma's sweet scent fills me. Scenes flash through my mind—her laughter, our tea parties, the cup slipping from her grasp. Tears fill my eyes, but I let the emotions ripple through me.

Finally, I take my hand away from the teacup and sigh. "It worked."

"What was it like?" Lily asks quietly.

"Incredible. I could see Grandma and smell her like she was here and hugging me. Kind of sad, but personal too."

Lily pushes off the doorframe and kneels beside me. "Every object has a story like people do. Some can be gentle, and some can be ... harsher."

I nod and turn to the baseball glove beside the teacup. "Like this one?"

"Yes." Her voice shakes with constrained emotion. "The boy who wore this didn't ... he didn't have an easy life."

"Can I see?"

"Yes."

I told her to stop protecting me at every turn, and she's finally listening. I reach out and place my palm over the glove. The boy's past flashes in a wave of sensations—the sting of a slap, the smell of cigarette smoke. The glove belonged to a young boy who dreamed about becoming a professional baseball player. He once had visions of a brighter future. But the brutality he experienced, the pain from his father's fists, and the burning sensation of his father's hatred changed everything. A desperate desire to escape replaced his aspirations for success. I recoil, cry out, and jerk my hand away. It's too much.

Lily pulls me in for a hug and holds me there. "The teacup was a start. But there are more things like this glove, Dee, and you have to shield yourself. Otherwise, you can get overwhelmed and drained."

I nestle into her embrace and comfort from the horror of the glove. "How? How can I stop the memories?"

She draws back, puts her hands on my shoulders, and stares into my eyes. "You stay focused and remember who you are. Keep a barrier in your mind, like a protective bubble. You can let the memories come when you touch something, but don't allow them to pierce your bubble."

I keep her words, and I practice for days. Each dirty attic relic turns into a lesson. After many mishaps, I filter and control my emotions, detach them, and turn them off if they become too much. I wouldn't appreciate how this training gave me much-needed strength until later. But whenever I endure bad memories from touch, I am thankful Lily took the time to do this with me.

Back in this cage, I run my fingers along the icy steel bars and sense the others' anguish. But before the feelings can engulf me, I remember the teacup, the glove, and Lily's words, which refuels my determination.

Lily may be gone, but my spirit? Not a freaking chance. The shadows of the past don't define me, nor does this cage.

"Hey." Cameron's voice rouses me. I lift my head as he approaches with a tray of food.

"You gotta eat, Delene."

I shake my head, turning away. "What's the point? You'll kill me anyway."

Cameron, looking confused, is young for an orderly—barely five years my senior. "Kill you? Why would we kill you?"

I gape, amazed. "How can you work here and be so naïve?"

Cameron sighs. "Look, can't you have a bite, and then you can get cleaned up? I don't want you to starve yourself."

Shifting the tray, he grips the bar with his free hand. An alarm goes off inside. This could be my opportunity.

I tilt my head, tracing my finger along his hand. "And if I do that…" He doesn't move, something flickering in his eyes. "If I take a bite, would you let me out for five minutes?"

"Delene, you know I can't."

I continue to stroke his hand, though he disgusts me. His past misdeeds slosh through my mind like dishwater. He kills animals and beats prisoners. He's never hurt me, but it takes every ounce not to cringe and pull away.

"Sure, you can," I purr. "Five tiny minutes and no one would ever know. I've been in this cage for two days. I'm cold, and I need to stretch." All right, my zero-flirting game is no secret. So, I mimic Lily's flirting and drop my voice to a soft tone. "I'd make it worth your while."

Cameron scans my eyes, and I gaze at him and let him think I return his demented crush. *Sure, dude, you have a chance of fulfilling whatever twisted fantasies roll around in your simian brain.* He chews his cheek, then sets the tray on the floor. I shift from foot to foot, wings tucked behind me.

Breathe, Delene.

Cameron lifts his key card and then pauses as he prepares to swipe. He gives me a warning glare. "I can get into a lot of trouble for this."

"Like I said, I'll make it worth your while."

He deliberates and swipes his card, and the buzzer goes off as the cell door opens. "Five minutes to stretch. Don't make me get out my baton."

"I won't." I'm lying, but this might be my only opportunity to escape.

Weak from starvation, I wobble out. Cameron's hand clasps around my elbow to prevent my fall. My first instinct is to yank away, but I let him help me stand, and I even thank him and dip my head as Lily did. Lily had flirting mastered. I'd look like I was flailing uncontrollably. He's not the brightest, but he's no fool either.

"Please give me a minute," I mutter. "To stretch."

He stands aside, folding his arms. "Make it quick."

"Okay."

I move a few feet into the center of the room, barefoot. The floor is empty, Cameron's desk off to the corner. I take a deep breath and let my wings unfurl. They span five feet in each direction. I stretch as far as possible, extend my arms, and release the tension in my shoulders. The weight of Cameron's eyes settles on me. His constant stare weirds me out. There's something not right with him.

I stretch my arms over my head as my feathers splay and survey the vaulted ceiling. There are a few places where I could fly and figure out what to do. I raise my wings.

"Don't fly," he warns.

I give him an innocent glance. "But if I don't, my muscles will atrophy."

His eyes widen. "They will?"

"Yes, like if you had to crouch in a closet for two days straight in the same position. I've got to move around. I will be good," I lie. Before Cameron protests, I fly fifteen feet to the ceiling. I land on the thick pipe and survey the room below me. I'm still lightheaded, but moving and being free is refreshing.

Below, Cameron paces with his lips pressed tightly in irritation. "Okay, you've flown around. Come here and have something to eat so I can take you back to your cage. I could get into serious trouble for this."

I spy a candy bar on his desk. "I will. Please give me a minute more. Hey, want to see something cool?"

"Not really. I want you to get back down here. You'll get me in trouble."

I dive, swoop over his desk, and snatch the candy bar.

"Hey," he shouts, "that's *mine*."

I laugh for the first time in months. "Not anymore, slow poke." I return to my perch on the thick pipe. I rip off the wrapper with my teeth and let the foil flutter to the floor as I sink into the sweetness. There is no way I will eat the lab food because I'm ninety-nine percent sure the food is drugged. The candy bar's chocolate, caramel, and nutty taste sends me an unexpected zing of energy. The chocolate's old, but I don't care. I devour it like a goblin. He shouts angrily, but I ignore him and eat the candy bar.

Heavily guarded soldiers stand outside the double doors in the far corner, and I need his key card to get through. There are no visible air vents around the ceiling.

"Delene, I'm not messing around. Get your wings down here, *now*."

I wave him on dismissively, which makes him even madder.

"I'm coming." No, I'm not.

I spot a hole in the ceiling along the opposite wall, where wires snake up the side and disappear above. I'm small, and I could fit in there. I'll get in trouble either way, but this is my one chance. Velcro rips as he unholsters his weapon. I meet his eyes as he lifts his gun and aims. "Don't," he growls. "It's a long way to go, even for you."

Too late. I squeeze through, scraping against the wires as bullets ping off the metal below. Gunpowder stings my nostrils as bullets whistle by. Fear leaves a metallic taste in my mouth.

Yeah, *right*, this guy doesn't want to hurt me.

I shimmy my way through the confined space against the complex wires. At the top, I emerge into a vast attic with electrical equipment and tall conduits. No one is here, but shouts and shots echo from below.

Frantic, I scan left and right and spot a closed window. I fly there. The window's small, but I could fit through, barely. The problem is its bulletproof glass.

"Come on, come *on*." As footsteps pound the stairwell, I search around, desperate for something to break through the glass.

There's a large wrench on the table. I don't see anything else thick enough to do the job, so I scoop the tool off the desk and fly, staring at the window from twenty feet away. *Come on.* I square my shoulders, flap, and barrel roll to the window.

I throw the wrench in the center and careen to the side. The wrench clatters to the floor, but it works. I check the window, where spiderwebs crack the glass. *Come on, one more.* I retrieve the wrench, fly twenty feet, and attack the window again. The wrench disappears out the window, along with the glass.

At the same time, the attic door bursts open, and Dr. Lytle's men rush in, their weapons pointed. I zoom for the window, desperate. Smashing through what's left of the glass, I free-fall into the paralyzing cold, then unfold my wings. The abrupt drag nearly rips my shoulders from their sockets.

I furiously beat the night sky, navigating the city's maze through blurry eyes. My thigh burns where the tranquilizer dart protruded minutes earlier, my head swimming against the drugs threatening to overtake me. Nerves jangling, I crest the city wall in a surge of adrenaline, leaving Dr. Lytle's nightmare behind. The towering concrete walls stretch fifty feet into the sky, fortifying the human city they call Refuge. Watchtowers loom at regular intervals, bristling with searchlights and automated cannons to deter potential enemies. Any outsiders steer clear of these formidable defenses.

But freedom awaits on borrowed time—I need to reach the mountains before the drugs drag me under. I push my wings to their limits, the black night my only ally.

Lights go on, and an alarm blares. I crest the lip of the wall, heading for the Wasatch Mountains in the distance, where I'll be safe. I fly as fast as I can. A white-hot jolt of pain rips through me. I notice a crossbow arrow piercing my wing, blood staining the feathers. *Oh no.*

Chapter Three

River

Tonight is quiet. I gnaw jerky and watch the stars, remembering Pops reading in the bunker. He loved language as much as the stars, calling them *luminous and celestial* with his plain-spoken eloquence.

The stars appear close enough to pluck, and I remember tracing shapes in the night sky with my brother on rooftops, away from Pops's ears. My twin brother Porter was my opposite—when I was serious, he lightened any situation and balanced me out. I still haven't gotten over the last time I saw him alive.

Months ago, my brother and I gathered supplies in a cornfield. We'd been on our own for a few years after Pops passed. Despite occasional disagreements, my brother was understanding and patient with me. The corn's lush, sweet, earthy smell put me at ease.

The wind roared as Porter dangled, tranquilized in a net as they hauled him away.

I don't know if they were aware of me or even knew I was there. I don't think so because they would've taken me, too. It would have been a bona fide harvesting deal. *Bargain.* I tried to get Porter loose but had no knife to cut the rope with. I flew behind the drones and followed them, but I had trouble when they spotted me. I almost got shot, and I've hidden here from that point on.

Most people who go to the lab don't come back. I've heard rumors about repetitive harvesting, and some are kept barely alive for blood, a crop of comatose vegetables.

Pops said the Stockade's sterile white halls house nightmarish technology manipulated by amoral scientists. Glass tubes filled with unfamiliar specimens line the walls. Robotic arms assist in medical procedures, handling serrated blades and harsh chemicals with uncaring precision.

Pops believed in the general goodness of people. He told me everyone is good at our roots, buried below the trivialities of humanity. I respected him more than anyone, but I struggle to believe *everyone* is good.

I drift off and stare at the stars, grateful I at least have food.

The faint blare of sirens sounds. I sit up, crane my neck, and listen. Something is going on.

I dust off the dirt and stand. I pull Pops's bomber jacket from the army tighter over my white T-shirt. My clothes need a good wash, but so do I. I finger my hair, closely cropped in the back, hot mess on top. Porter wore his long. I made slits in Pop's jacket a while back for my wings, but it fits right and keeps me covered. The sirens get louder. I freeze, listening. The noise is close. I double-tie my boots over my fatigues and tuck the laces in. I can't afford to trip when hunting and on the run. I turn to the west, where searchlights crossbeam over the canyon. Okay, west is a no-go.

I curse, chuck my blanket with the food, and jam jerky and nuts into my bag, casting furtive glances west. I could hide out in the lean-to, but if they flew here, they'd catch me. East, then, or hide in the trees below.

No matter—they're coming.

I secure the pouch, run to the plateau, and fly.

Chapter Four

Delene

Hit and plummeting, I lurch forward, dodging gunfire.

I gasp as my injured wing sags, and I'm thrown like a rag doll in the wind, somersaulting toward the ground. I'm close to the mouth of the canyon. On the verge of blacking out, I battle to stay aloft despite the pain. I gain temporary altitude, soaring a few hundred feet closer to the mountains.

Vehicles din below. Searchlights flash across my back. I keep flying as long as I am able. The stream snakes out of the mountain and flows into a lake at the mouth of the canyon.

If I can get there, I can hide in the forest. My wing cramps, and I drop at least a hundred feet until I catch an updraft, then coast on the wind again.

Trying to speed up proves difficult. I'm losing blood, and I may not ever fly again.

"Come on," I growl through gritted teeth. "Almost there."

As I near the lake's edge, my body decides to give up. I close my wings inward and dive diagonally toward the water.

If I die, it will be on my terms. They will not torture and harvest me. I topple against branches, which whip and cut. I plunge into icy waters, barely conscious. A thousand knives stab my wing as I sink. My toes touch soft mud at the bottom. I squat and kick hard, propelling to the surface.

They're coming.

I gasp for air, tread water, and swim to the shore when I reach the surface. Blood drips over my shoulder, staining my white jumpsuit. My wing's busted, and I'm soaked. I crawl onto the rocky beach and lay on my side, gasping.

My fingers close around the thin, streamlined metal of the lodged arrow, but I hesitate. If the arrow pierces a blood feather, it'll siphon my blood, and I will bleed out. But if I don't try, I'll die. I release the arrow and grab the hem of my jumpsuit leg, wet and pasted to my skin. I brace against the agony and rip the hem half past my calf. I tear the fabric into long strips. I'll have to stop the blood.

I set the strips next to me and touch the arrow again, dread filling me. I hate self-induced pain. I'm tough, but I've *always* hated self-induced pain.

This is going to hurt.

Before I can second-guess myself, I yank the arrow hard, dropping the remains to the pebbles. A wave of pain ricochets through me, and I might faint for a second. I don't, so I grab the strips of cloth and bind the wound as best I can, making a tight double field strip with another slip of fabric. I rock back and forth and will the pain to subside so I can at least think.

The throbbing in my shoulder stops, and I tie my wet hair back into a low ponytail with another strip. The sirens from the valley intensify, and I labor to get to my feet. I'm freezing, wet, and in pain, and I look like a Fae hobo with a horrible fashion sense who lost a bet with a sidewalk. But I'm alive. I grit my teeth and stand.

Sharp and uneven rocks press again into the soles of my feet. I wobble, looking at the looming mountain. It's high and shoots straight into the sky.

One thing I'm good at is climbing. I can't see anything in the moonlight, but my arms and legs still work. And I can still climb. Though my back muscles burn like fire, I limp to the foot of the mountain.

I use my fist as a cam the way Dad taught me, and I wedge my fist between a crack for leverage as I find footing. *You stupid, suicidal numpty.* I go slow. I might escape, but if they shine a spotlight on me, they'll catch me.

My wings and hair will stand out against the mountain like a snowball in the mud. But this is my only choice. Reality hits me: I'm fighting a losing battle but won't stop. My best bet is to get as high as possible, where they won't follow.

My wet toes, caked with mud, slip on the rocks as I climb, determined to escape. I slip and fight to grasp the handholds. Resolute, I keep going. I won't go out like my sister. She believed peace was the answer, but these people aren't interested in peace. They're interested in harvesting our blood so they can live.

When I fly, I relax my shoulders and let aerodynamics work in tandem. The sharp wing-pull tenses my shoulders. My arms and legs work, but reaching and lifting brings agony. I pull up using both my hands and feet. I go slow, but the intense pull burns like a hot iron.

My shoulders ache as I lift them repeatedly, determined to reach the top.

More. A little higher.

I focus on one rock at a time, grip hard, and jam my fist into crevices. I've scraped my hands, and my knuckles bleed, but I push forward.

After a while, I'm high. My dad taught me never to look down, and I'm not about to. I'm a sweaty mess near the top, searching for a secure handhold. I touch something solid and slippery. I lose my balance, dangling over a hundred feet up, clinging to the rock.

Gulping down air, I struggle to regain my footing. I slap the sweat off my jumpsuit and lunge toward the rock again. This time, I close my hand over a handhold and push into my footrests.

I suck in the air and rest my forehead against the mountain: *Delene, you fool.* I'm going to fall to my death. They're going to catch me and gut me like a fish.

My breath becomes labored. I inhale and concentrate on what I'm doing with my hands and feet. Panic and pain threaten to end me, but I push through. I climb until my head reels and my hand meets a flat surface.

My eyes widen, and I lift my head over the edge to a flat plateau.

Every joint and muscle is on fire, but I pull my body weight up, roll over, and collapse onto the plateau, panting. My hands are scraped and raw from the climb.

A light breeze blows against my neck. I cry. In captivity, I hid my vulnerability to stay strong.

But I let loose for making it to the top of this crazy mountain, for Lily, for Mom and Dad. I'm wracked with sobs, my chest heaving, and for once, I don't care. I hate the unfairness of being ousted in a world where everyone has already lost so much. I may die here, in this remote, high spot. My damaged wing bleeds through the cloth strip, and upheaval depletes me.

"I'm sorry," I rasp. *I'm sorry, Lily, for not being able to help. I'm sorry I got shot and will most likely die overnight. I'm sorry I couldn't stop Dr. Lytle from hurting others.*

I take a big gulp of air. Eventually, my breathing slows, and the tears subside. Lily and I spun as kids until we collapsed, the world a blur.

The same sensation overtakes me.

Chapter Five

River

I fly at breakneck speed.

If I stay, I'm a sitting duck on a silver platter. I built my nest too high for them. Equipment malfunctions, the air gets thinner, and it's not the ideal location for anyone—but Evol-humans. When they come into the mountains, they're here for a purpose. Some of us hide in an abandoned ski lodge, cave, cabin, or the forest. And they get caught every time.

But they'll notice me if they bring the choppers this way, looking for whoever they're searching for.

I keep moving.

The growling engines drive me on as I stay hidden, navigating the woods, scanning, and tracking. Below, two black SUVs stop on the roadside. I listen hard, staying concealed.

Armed guards get out and patrol near the tailgate.

"Like I done told ya, she crashed right into that lake. Ain't no way she survived. I'd wager my rations we'll find her corpse at the bottom."

The other replies, "Flynn scanned it already. *Nada*. We'll search all night, so move."

Gravel crunches beneath their combat boots as they walk. "Why is this one so important, anyway?" the first guy grumbles. "Can't the doc use the others in the holding cells?"

"There's no one left, numbnuts. Anyway, the doc said this one's special. Move out."

I wait until the voices fade. Then I fly into the forest, high above the trees—unseen, unspotted. I can't risk the nest, but even so, I can't stay there. I might as well advertise an Evol-human on a diamond-encrusted platter slathered in barbecue sauce.

I scan the trees. They're searching for a "her." Could another Evol-human be close by?

As night falls, more soldiers come. I find a safe hideout in an old aspen, concealed by thick branches and impressive height.

Hiding often wears on me.

Dawn grows close, but the sun hasn't risen yet. I readjust on the rough branch, bark flakes digging in. Far below, birds chirp faintly. Squirrels rustle in the underbrush—the single sign of life apart from the soldiers' periodic voices.

I regret not bringing a blanket. I have leftover matches but no fire. My body's cold, my mouth dry and thirsty. My fingers are limp noodles about to fall off. I drape over the thick branch, resting my head on the trunk as I survey the ground below.

Chapter Six

Delene

Pain flares as I open my crusted eyes. The sunlight stains the world red. I brush away the grit, hoping it's not blood. Slowly, my surroundings sharpen. I'm wet, cold, and alive.

Glancing sideways, I gasp.

Not an inch away, a sheer cliff jettisons sharply, plunging hundreds of feet below. Nausea grips me. I can't believe I climbed so high in the dark. Memories of pushing past unbearable pain to reach this ledge rush back. I remember continuing until the pain was too much to bear. After I hauled onto the ledge, I collapsed. If I'd known how high I was or the lack of actual handholds and footrests, I'd have plummeted to my death, no question.

Taking a deep breath, I steady my frantically pounding heart, then wince as my drained, sluggish body protests. Recollections of frantically searching for handholds, the terror of near-falls, and sheer exhaustion play in my mind like a slideshow.

I don't know what to expect, but whoever lives here will be back. Or maybe gone for good. If I'm lucky, I can recuperate here.

I have no memory of blacking out, which scares me. How much blood have I lost? My head spins, but the pain keeps me grounded.

Lifting my elbow, I take in the scene: a ledge with an old, partially deflated air mattress beneath me. Three fallen pines are stacked to the right, seemingly unused for firewood.

Repositioning myself, I grimace. There's no way I can fly. I can barely lift my wing. I gather my strength and scramble into a sitting position.

My hands, raw and cut from the climb, throb in agony. It hurts to open and close them. Funny how you can go with workable joints and take your body parts for granted until a part fails.

Snowy peaks glisten in the distance. I'd be in business if I had a slight dusting of snow to ease my palm's burning. My toes are numb, and my left foot pulsates.

I sit cross-legged and examine my feet. They're even worse, cut and bloodied from the rocks. I pluck embedded pebbles and take in the haunting beauty around me.

The canyons have a spooky vibe in the morning light. Wispy clouds encircle the mountaintops. A refreshing drizzle permeates the sweet, earthy pines. A thin silver stream snakes through the pine-filled valley far below, leading toward the abandoned remains of a small town—lopsided wooden buildings with broken windows, rusted cars, and appliances scattered in the streets like discarded toys.

This place is a haven.

The secluded camp is meticulously organized, with a neat fire pit of flat, clean stones framing burned logs. I shift the air mattress from the cliff's edge and clean and bandage my feet. I can stand, but it hurts.

Nearby, two lidded, airtight plastic containers sit under a natural rock overhang. Curiosity piqued, I lift one lid: dried jerky. The other holds foraged forest roots and nuts. There's enough food here to last me for weeks or months. Someone stocked these containers for an extended stay.

Aside from my dent, the air mattress looks unused. I slide nearer, wincing, to the small fire pit. A natural stone awning creates a small, shady lean-to.

Everything's orderly here. There's a bucket next to the lean-to, and I'm curious about its deal. Opting for a more rustic approach by the pines, I dig a hole, cover it up, and leave the bucket out of the equation—no need to bother.

The covered area is not large enough to sleep in but would supply shelter during a storm. It's secluded and safe.

My stomach growls, fed up with me.

Excited by using my ability, I touch the plastic water jug, refreshing after so long without touching anything innocent. As I close my eyes, I sense the pure flow of stream water. Putting my hand on the cage before was hard because I felt the pain of past prisoners. This is something else — total immersion. The jug's positive energies are lovely.

My stomach rumbles again. While I've endured hunger, often for self-preservation, I eagerly tear into the jerky. I consume three strips and savor the authentic, fresh taste.

Stealing blurs the line between right and wrong, but desperation justifies my theft. If I don't eat, I'll die.

I stop as soon as I finish the third jerky strip. I'll take what I need and find some way off here. If I can recover for a day, I may be able to fly over the mountain. But I have nowhere to go.

Pain consumes me, and I brace myself against the rock wall, leaning my forehead on it. *Please, please let this pain end.*

A misty afternoon fog rolls in and creeps through the mountains. The mist helps conceal me, even this high up. But I can't get warm. I do my best to move and circulate my arms and legs, but I'm limited in how much I can move around.

I eat some jerky and chestnuts, washing them down with water. I don't take more than I need.

My body needs to readapt, and if someone lives here, they won't take kindly to my plowing through their food.

I rinse the blood off my hands and scrub clean. I don't want to waste water, but I rinse them again to be sure. Dad warned us about airborne pathogens. I'm more conscious of this now than when I was with Lily because she cared for me, and I didn't think for myself quite as much.

My throat tightens at the memory of Dr. Lytle strolling to my cage, telling me about the complications and apologizing for

Lily's death. He acted so calm and collected. Has he ever had a family, brother, sister, or someone he loved and lost? Everyone I've met at the lab has seemed emotionally removed, as if their souls have taken off. At the same time, they continued with their work like mindless zombies.

The sun spans farther across the valley. They'll have difficulty breathing in places harder for humans, so the nest should be okay. Natural fliers have an easier time surviving the higher altitudes. I'm at least safe.

I'm still dizzy and don't know how much blood I've lost. It's chilly but not as cold as last night. Lily often remarked that when the cold penetrates deep into your bones, winter is coming.

Snow tops the distant mountains. This one's not far behind.

The fire pit would barely fit a sundial, and I don't understand how the rocks work. The rocks' shape is precise and flat, like pondstones. They aren't cliff rocks, that's for sure. Smoothing the stone, I try to understand. Maybe it's spiritual. Different faiths have sprung up over the decades. Some deluded people even worshiped Evol-humans as angels. Lily and I joked because we were about as angelic as gargoyles as children. I still can't figure out the stones.

I search for flint but can't light a fire. There's enough food to sustain me until I decide what to do. I eat and sleep—no clues in the sky except an ocean of clouds. Evol-humans heal quickly, and a few days here should help me recover.

I slide nearer on the rough, red clay, the ground's jagged edges scraping my skin beneath the shreds of my pants. The clay dirt is dusty but fertile, traces of abandoned farms and homesteads plowed into this valley long before the world's end. I trail my fingers over the smooth, air-soft top mattress, searching for clues.

Shadows drape over the mountains, zigzagging like laundry lines. Memories of Lily's carefree smile and sunny spirit fill me. No matter where we were, she found joy. I wish I had her resilience. As the clouds part above the nest, warm sunlight spills over me. My toes curl against the stone, muscles soaking up the sun's warmth after so long trapped indoors. Out here, I'm at the mercy of Mother Nature's whims.

I force myself to stay awake, battling dizziness, fatigue, malnourishment, and blood loss.

Wrapped in a coarse but warm blanket found with the food, I lean against the rock and surrender to sleep.

Chapter Seven

River

Fantastic. Sun's back and the nest has a perfect fire and stones. But I'm unable to use them. I have to hide, listening to these two clowns—the soldiers from last night smoke at the tree's base.

"Why are we here, man?"

"Following orders. Don't ask."

The shorter guy drops a heavy duffel. "CO said we'll be out as long as it takes. Quartermaster dropped these for doubles."

My eye catches the black bag he kicks near the foot of the tree.

"Eh, we won't be here for long. We'll handle this and bag 'em and tag 'em."

"So, you think she's dead?"

"Think about it. The girl fell a long way, and they already shot her."

My eyes narrow. His flippant, casual tone grates me. They go to great lengths to take our blood, then act like our deaths would be more convenient for them in the long run. I could never value my life above another's.

"Well, let's hope you're right for the girl's sake *and* ours. I don't want to spend more than a day here."

"Same. Hey, have you met him? The big guy?"

"Who, Dr. Lytle?"

"Yeah, man."

"No. I saw the doc in passing. I'm a grunt."

"Consider yourself lucky, then."

"Why? He is bad, as they say?"

"You don't even know." The second guy lowers his voice. I strain to hear them. "He looks normal, right? Like a *nice guy* and always whistles a song like he's right where he wants to be, without care."

"I haven't had a chance to talk to him."

"He's a monster. I've seen him do the unthinkable. And those pale eyes of his? They ain't *intense,* man. They've got poison in them, like black oil."

The forest falls silent, and I'm worried they spotted me. But the second man whistles low. "Well, good thing we're on the winning side and not against *him*, right?"

The trees reverberate with the sound of his reloading rifle. "Yeah, good thing."

I press deeper into the rough bark, barely daring to breathe as the soldiers' voices drift up. Craning my neck, I glimpse their glowing ember tips as they pass a cigarette back and forth. *How much longer?* Their languid complaints blend and my thoughts focus only on their imminent departure.

Last night's cold felt like a knife's edge without the warming rocks. By now, the stones will have grown icy and useless, unable to provide their usual heat. *Great.* Another frigid, comfortless night. I grit my teeth against the chill already sinking into my bones.

Just go already, I plead silently, shifting from foot to foot to keep warm. At last, the soldiers grind the cigarettes out and continue their patrol. I exhale once the forest sounds return, breath clouding the air. I have to get back before nightfall. If I can't return to the nest by this afternoon, another night here will suck.

I ration the jerky and scrape at the bark. Spotting a loose flap on the pine trunk, I pull it back to unveil the moist inner layer. There is no visible fungus, and the bark appears healthy, so I inspect the cambium layer next to the wood.

Pops took time to teach Porter and me survival skills in the wild when I was younger. He said that during his time in the army, he learned that you can't predict where you'll end up, and mastering survival skills makes the difference between life and death. He was right. Here, there *is* no coasting. You either know what you're doing, or you die.

He taught me to boil and fry bark from certain trees, ensuring I knew which ones were poisonous and how to eat bark raw in desperate situations. The texture is thick as I roll it around in my mouth. The nutrients will give me the needed calories. The flavor is bland, like cardboard. Still, food is food.

Pops was a survival expert who taught Porter and me to distinguish edible mushrooms from poisonous ones and find safe berries. Born in wartime, he ensured our safety and knowledge. I was always closer to Pops. He cared deeply, especially after our mom passed and Dad changed. By two, Dad's carelessness had cost him his life.

Out here, there's no code or rules of etiquette. *Have compassion for others, hold on to your principles, give thanks to God, and be faithful*, Pops used to say.

One day, he ran into a few of his old buddies from his unit while hunting. We were sixteen, and despite our bravado, the men scared us. They were loud, nonstop drunk, and high. Pops reassured us they were good guys and always had each other's backs, and no one got left behind in his unit. He offered to help them, but the men turned on him and put a bullet through his head, leaving us and stealing his belongings.

I haven't trusted anyone except Porter for several years.

I wished to share Pops's faith in humanity, but his optimism cost him dearly. I knew those men were evil. Their repugnance grated my bones. Pops tried to stay sane and clutch onto some fragment of decency, but I hesitate to trust so easily. You never know who you'll run into.

Porter and I were born five years on the tail of the Scourge outbreak, a botched viral weapon that went global. Pops said the intended attack spiraled out of control, toppling nations in days. We belong to the second generation of Evol-humans, formed on our devastated Earth.

Great job, guys. Sarcastic mental applause all around.

I turn my neck when there's a hiss to my right. Less than a foot away, a cougar bares its teeth. I'm anchored to the spot as we lock stares.

"Should we take the drones higher, scan the cliffs?" The men chat below. "We've searched the valley, still no sign."

"No. The girl's injured. Matheson shot her. She's in the trees or bushes if she isn't dead. There's no *way* that girl will fly with a broken wing. I'm telling you, she's right under our noses. I bet she's nearby right now."

The cougar growls low and advances. I stumble back and lose my footing. I try to grab the tree trunk, but it's too late. I fall.

Branches whip at my cheek and scratch my arms.

I beat against the wind and land on the forest floor. I crouch and spread my wings to either side of me. Leaves crunch nearby, and I pivot my attention, wide-eyed, at the backs of the soldiers.

They haven't noticed me. I stand rooted.

"I noticed you talking to Ullrich this morning. Looked heated."

"It was. I've had enough of Ullrich and told the idiot so."

I slow down and step lightly. If I attempt to fly away, they'll hear and shoot.

The taller soldier shakes his head and scoffs. "Not what it looked like to *me.*"

"Well, it was. I said, if you think I'm going to take your BS, man, you got another think coming. I don't care if you *are* my superior officer."

"*Oh?*" The shorter guy scoffs. "And what did he say?"

"Oh, we had words."

"You had *words.* Right. Were these words, 'go clean the latrine?'"

"Screw you, Johnson. I'm telling you, man. I told him off."

"Uh-huh." The soldier doesn't sound like he's buying it, nor am I.

The cougar stares, then licks its chops. I can't exactly fly to get away from these bozos. If they spot me, I'm dead. I don't want to be the cougar's brunch, either, so I'm screwed.

I hug the tree trunk, paralyzed, as the cougar snarls. Once, when I was a kid, Pops brought me to these mountains, and we tracked a buck as a storm rolled in.

"*Get down,*" Pops had shouted over a boom of thunder. When the winds hit, we ducked beneath a rocky outcropping, and harsh gusts stripped branches from oscillating trees. I'd huddled against Pops's sturdy frame. He shielded me as debris whizzed past.

After endless minutes, the gale calmed. Pops clapped my shoulder, his weathered hand lingering. *"We'll ride it out together, River. Ain't nothing you can't handle if you use your wits."*

His words echo as the cougar creeps closer, fixated on me with predatory hunger. I struggle to think clearly. What would Pops do? I envision his calm, steady presence and gravelly voice like warm milk.

I may stand alone, but the skills he instilled carry me forward. I track the cougar's movements with quiet focus and let instinct take over.

The cougar decides now's the best time in the world to announce his presence to everybody. He growls loudly, and the roar reverberates. The cougar pounces, and I let go, then tumble through whipping branches. I land in a crouch. My wings spread wide, and I grip my knife as the cougar circles hungrily.

The men whirl around in alarm, and their attention falls on me.

Uh-oh.

I freeze as all eyes turn my way. With a nonchalant shrug, I offer a casual "'Sup?" But my muscles coil, ready to fight or take flight.

The shorter guy draws his weapon, and before I have the chance to blink or fly away, a bullet whizzes past my ear. Well, thank God he sucks at marksmanship. The cougar takes off through the trees at the gunfire.

I swipe the duffel bag and run. The bag is light, allowing me to sprint at full speed. I lose the soldiers and pause. A cave opening catches my eye about a hundred feet away along the mountain wall. I turn back, listening for the men.

Nothing. Not even footsteps. They must have thought I went a different way.

I think I lost them. I lick my lips, cold and chapped, and I swallow dryly. It's a gamble, running into the mouth of the cave. But either I enter the cave, risk a wrestling match with a bear or the cougar's cubs, or stay here and become a science experiment.

Yeah, I'll take the cave, thanks.

I unsheathe my knife and dart through the narrow, jagged gap. Emerging on the other side, I whoop.

This cave is the ultimate jackpot. Oh yeah, this is a perfect spot. The EMP killer works for the most part, but Pops said it could be glitchy. I'm safer here until they capture whoever they're after.

I untie my satchel and smile as I take in my surroundings. Perfect. I'll lie low here and fly back tonight.

Chapter Eight

Delene

Delene.
Delene, wake up.

Lily's voice stirs me. Confusion sets in as I open my eyes, and the cold pierces my damp clothes. My dreams often feature Lily. Always Lily. My parents had their share of concerns. My mother was preoccupied with ensuring our next meal and our safety. My bond with Lily always felt stronger. Throughout my youth, she was not just my sister but also my closest companion.

The dreams in the lab filled me with dread, aware as I was of her passing. Now, memories of her smile, her freckled nose, and the twinkle in her blue eyes—so much like mine—comfort me. I have no photographs, but her image remains vivid and cherished.

Hunger pangs strike, and pain twists in my stomach. I move toward the food drums to consume jerky and wild nuts. After such a long period without food, this newfound cache is almost irresistible.

But it's not right, especially if the person here will return. I sip water and reclose the containers.

The air mattress is flat. I roll off, kneel, uncap the plastic lid, and blow air into the bed like a drunk trumpet player until it's full. I recap the lid, lay back, and turn away from the sunlight. The scratchy, thin material does nothing to protect me from the cold wind.

If the blanket was all the people who lived here had, how did they stay warm? I circulate my arms and legs beneath the wool and rub my palms together. I could get a fire going if I had some matches or a lighter.

The view from the mountaintop is breathtaking. I see why someone chose to camp here. A cool breeze brushes my skin, and I gaze across the vast mountain range. The muted autumn hues are turning brown, signaling winter's approach.

A stream winds through the valleys, and the hidden city lies beyond the western ridge.

The gust picks up, and I cross my arms for warmth. I have no idea what time it is, but the sun sinks low in the west and seems later in the day, close to evening. Given my food, water, and bed, I shouldn't complain. On family journeys, we often had even less. I survey the distant snowcapped mountains, grateful to be alive. How long before the snow arrives if I stay hidden? If I fly again, perhaps I'll steal something to light a fire. My search around the campsite didn't yield much. Whoever was here took all manner of weapons and kindling.

A red splotch in my side vision distracts me. The bandage soaks through again.

Frustrated, I tear the hem of my untouched pantsuit leg. Even though I'm cold and could use fire, I make bandage strips like I did with the other one. After removing my dressing, I retrieve the water, pour a splash over the wound, and wince as white-hot pain sweeps over me.

Tying a clean strip, I stop the bleeding.

The sun is setting. I nestle into the blanket, covering my face with my wing, and with a full belly, I doze off.

Chapter Nine

River

I swoop into camp, halting abruptly. A stranger lies in my bed, small and dirty like Goldilocks fell through quicksand. I approach cautiously, dagger ready. Appearances deceive. If she escaped pursuit, she's clever and capable.

I stand still as stone and take in the girl's tangled halo of blonde hair and delicate wings under a ragged blanket. She's wounded, caked with blood and mud, her hand blistered raw. It's hard to tell how deep her wound goes or if she has more. I tilt my head and forget to breathe.

I can't stop staring at her lips. She's beautiful—pale skin, nice cheekbones. Like a doll.

Her chest rises and falls. So, she's alive.

My eyes dart to my food supplies, where the girl threw the lids and trash on the floor, disturbing the pine needles I placed for insect protection. I curse under my breath and put the lids back on. Great, here come the ants. Her carelessness irritates me. If Porter did that, I'd freak out.

I glance again at the girl.

She clutches the blanket around her shoulders. I watch her for too long, but I can't help it. If you notice another of your kind around, you're curious to learn all about them.

And she isn't hard on the eyes.

One or two other males came to the forest a couple of months ago and were hunted and caught. Unless you're family, we tend to keep to ourselves. The price on our heads is too high to risk anyone else's life. But she's different. I stop in front of her, closer.

There are no visible weapons, but I touch her shoulder warily.

"Hey. Lady. Time to rise and shine," I say gravelly, trying to rouse her.

The girl inhales sharply, grimacing, and her eyes open, a deep, royal blue. She scampers back against the cliff wall, clutching the blanket. "Who are you?"

"I could ask you the same question," I reply smoothly, raising an eyebrow. "Name's River. River Shaw. And just who are you trespassing in my nest?"

Chapter Ten

Delene

I wake to a muscular, silent figure looming over me, his wings casting unnerving shadows. Intelligent dark eyes scrutinize me from his smooth, brown face framed by cropped black hair and raven quills. He's been around the block.

My guard shoots up. I'd stand, but my body's too weak from the climb. "*Your* nest, huh? Sorry, I didn't see your name on it."

"It's carved right over there." He points past me to the rockface. My eyes travel over the stone, where he'd etched *River* in craggy letters. The carved name is so tiny I didn't notice.

"Now you're supposed to tell me *your* name. That's how this goes."

I blink. "Delene Fairborne. Listen, would you mind if I— *ow*," I scrape against the wall and suck air through my teeth. I clamp my eyes shut.

"Are you okay?"

I shrug the blanket off, and my injured wing flops lamely near my shoulder. River's eyebrows lower, and he comes closer. "Let me look."

He stows his serrated hunting knife, presents empty hands, and crouches to examine my injury. "Relax. I won't hurt you. Let's see the damage." He's gentle, avoiding the wound and handling my feathers softly. He lightly touches the bandage.

"Dr. Lytle runs the Stockade, the underground bunker and lab where the humans imprison and experiment on our kind. His men hunted me down and shot me with a crossbow as I tried to escape. The wound is still healing—I changed the bandage earlier, but without a spare set of clothes, I had to tear strips off my pants to re-dress it."

"Hmm." He examines the back with a frown. "There's an exit wound."

"Yeah, I pulled it out."

"Well, that was stupid of you. You could have died if those goons pierced a blood feather."

My temper flares. "Oh, as opposed to leaving it in. I'd rather take my chances, thanks." My voice is hostile, though I'm grateful for his help. I still don't know who he is or what he wants, and my mother warned me to be on my guard.

River sits back on his haunches, sighs, and meets my eyes. "Doesn't look good. How long have you been here, kid? A day or so?"

"I'm no kid. I'm seventeen."

"Well, I'm *eighteen*. So, you're a kid."

"By what, a few whole months?" I snicker. "Okay. If a *kid* free-climbed in the pitch-black up a hundred-foot cliff to get here, I guess I'm a kid."

After examining the wound, he says, "The damage looks fixable. Let's clean this well to prevent infection."

"I've *cleaned* the wound."

"Clean *deeper*," he admonishes. "I don't have antibiotics, but I'll try to get some. Or at least honey. Honey heals."

He hesitates before retrieving water, then takes a rag from his pouch and soaks the cloth. With the knife still in hand, he comes closer.

"Look … You seem all right, but I'm a lone wolf. I operate solo. You have a target with a big 'X' on your back. I feel bad for you. I do. But you know how it is with our kind." He gives me a blatant look, so *here's your cue to leave.*

"Gee, I'd kindly vacate the premises, but I can't *fly*."

He rubs the back of his neck, agitated. "The valley's full of drones. And they've got at least a dozen soldiers combing the forest."

"I'm sorry." I shift my eyes down. "You never asked for any of this."

"None of us did," he waves me off. "The soldiers are here. I'm screwed either way." He pauses and assesses me. "Stay the night. Then after that, I'm sorry, but you need to find somewhere else to hide."

The night might be all I need. "Thank you."

"It's too late to light a fire, so we'll have to rough it and light one in the morning." He scratches the back of his neck, pivots, and returns to the unlit fire. "Tonight's going to get cold."

I stare at the barren plateau, desperation rising. "What exactly did you expect me to light a fire with? Two sticks and a prayer?" I motion emphatically to the rocky emptiness.

River pauses, then reaches into his pocket, producing a matchbox. "I had these on me," he admits reluctantly. "But it's probably for the best. Heating those rocks takes hours."

His words land like a blow, and I turn away to hide frustrated tears. Swallowing down hurt and anger, I take a deep breath before facing him again. Survival always comes first. But his small act of neglect cuts deeper than I expected. I could have been warm last night. I'll need to be more self-reliant from here on out.

I note the flat rocks around the small fireplace. "What are they for, anyway?"

"They keep me warm at night." He pauses, regarding the crumpled wool on the air mattress. "Wait ... did you sleep with only the blanket last night?"

"I'm kind of short on options here."

River chews his cheek and nods. "We both are. Jeez, you must have been freezing."

"I'm all right." I push my hair back from my face. "I'm strong."

"I noticed." Something like respect shines in his dark eyes. "Let's get through the night and warm the rocks tomorrow. Why don't you go back to sleep and get rest? I'll eat and keep a lookout. We'll talk in the morning."

He turns away and busies himself, cleaning up the food barrels. My mind knots with guilt. Why wasn't I more careful, and why didn't I ensure the lids were tight? I lie there, watching him, and the inertia of the last few days pulls me to sleep.

I wake the next day to the early dawn, and River hovers over me with a concerned frown.

River's dark gaze lingers on me. I cross my arms with a huff. "What?"

He scoffs, the corners of his eyes crinkling. "Nothing. Just noticing you look like a ghost, that's all."

"My, your powers of observation are astounding."

His mouth twitches, and he shrugs his bomber jacket off, passing his wings through the slits.

"What are you doing?" I ask, alarmed. I don't remember anything after I conked out last night. Where did he sleep? *Did* he sleep?

"Whoa. Relax, Princess. I'm not that kind of man. When I said you look white, I'm not playing. You're pale as a ghost." He reaches his arm out, offering the jacket. "Put it on. It'll keep you warm."

I sit up and take the jacket, dipping my head. "What about you?"

He rubs his hands together. "I'll be fine. I'll get a fire going and find you a warmer outfit later. Here, let me help."

He fixes the jacket through my wings, tender and meticulous. The jacket's enormous, and the slits in the back pass through without worsening my injury. The soft sheepskin lining comforts me.

I nod my thanks. Dad said kindness isn't always free. Accepting River's help feels like a personal sacrifice. I tug the coat closer and blow warm air into my hands.

Oddly, I trust him.

He scratches his chin, eyeing the valley thoughtfully. "We'll stay here for a day or two until it blows over."

"You mean you'll let me stay?" My ears perk up.

"Maybe. But there are no guarantees."

"You're still miffed about the barrels, aren't you?"

He glances at me like he's irritated and shrugs, but there's a teasing twinkle in his eye.

"Sorry, I should have been tidier, but I was delirious. Hey, have helicopters ever come here?"

"No. It's too high and steep, and the equipment doesn't work. Signals go haywire, and reception's crap."

"How have you evaded their heat sensors for so long?"

River shakes his head and points to a high pine. "Did you notice that?"

I squint at the pine tree. "Notice what?"

"Three branches away from the trunk. The slightly raised bump. That box disrupts the helicopters' electronics." He roots around in his bag and extracts binoculars. "Take a look."

I lift the binoculars and zoom in on the tree. The blink-and-you'll-miss-it black box is so tiny I would have mistaken it for a pinecone or bark. "Awesome. Where did you get it?"

"Pops built it," he says. "In the army, he was a munitions engineer, an expert in his Ranger unit. I installed it after I got here."

"Cool." I hand the binoculars back to River. "And no other Evol-humans have come here?"

He shakes his head. "Two were on the run about a month ago but got caught."

"Oh…" I stare at the valley as my mind wanders. River's saving my life. He knows it, and I know it. I meet his eyes again. "What about drones? Could they make it this high?"

"The high-grade drones might if they're desperate enough, but most don't even reach halfway. Those things are glitchy."

I bob my head. Old and neglected, most of the equipment isn't as good anymore, but the weapons are still deadly.

I stand and join River at the plateau, tender-footed. Despite the warm jacket, my bones ache, and goosebumps rise on my arms. Trees conceal us, but I see vehicles below, faint figures. Are they planning something? Will they give up if they can't find me? Dr. Lytle is hungry for my blood. With most of us on the verge of extinction, there's no way he'd pack it in and say, *Oh well*. I shiver and hug my arms tightly.

He'll hunt me to the end. I'm aware of River's staring, and I sniff. "What?"

"I've been wondering, how'd you get up here? I know you didn't fly."

"I climbed." I bring the jacket's cuff up to my cold nose to get warm.

He doubts my feat. "You climbed *that*?"

I nod. "I happen to be a good climber."

"You *must* be."

An uneasy silence stretches between us. I tuck a loose strand of hair behind my ear, shifting from foot to foot. "Look, I know you said there are no guarantees to me staying, but isn't there a solution here? Please, I just need somewhere to hide, and I'll pull my weight."

He winces. "You'd be another mouth to feed."

"I sort of figured," I say. "But I'm not in any condition to leave, so if you're in such a hurry to get rid of me, go ahead and toss me over the cliff. Maybe the wind will kick up, and I'll land in the stream."

He makes a funny face like he isn't sure whether to laugh or pitch me over. He shakes his head, crouches by the fireplace, and taps the match as he inspects the empty kindling. "I've got eight matches left." He lights the kindling, then stands and pockets the matchbox. "Now there are seven. Come over here and get warm. Listen, since you offered to pull your weight, we might as well talk about it. You should earn your keep if you plan to stay."

I narrow my eyes. "And *what*, in your book, does one do to earn one's keep?" I don't disguise the mistrust in my voice. He might've joked about me being a kid, but I'm far from it. I'm well aware of what many younger women have had to do to "earn their keep," he should know I won't be earning my keep that way.

He's calm. "Chill, Lady Godiva. My grandfather raised me to respect a lady."

"Good. We're clear, then," I state bluntly. "Because I'm about as useful as a screen door on a submarine right now."

He laughs. "Look, chivalry aside … I meant you could do things around here to help. Collect rainwater, store and harvest food. You know, make yourself useful."

"Okay. That's fair, I'll help. Is that what the bucket's for, rainwater?" I toss my head in the direction of the bucket.

"Yeah. I also use it for cleaning. Fresh water only."

I drape the blanket over my lap, thankful for the fire's heat a few feet away. "Are the mornings here always this cold?"

He chuckles. "This ain't cold."

"It's not?"

He shakes his head. "No, it's *chilly*. In a few weeks, it'll get a *lot* colder. If you stay until you heal, I'll teach you how to smoke and store jerky, and you can help scrape hides if I get another deer. You know, *earn your keep*." His voice lilts with a hint of teasing.

I almost sass back, but I nod. "I'll contribute. You have my word."

"We have a deal, then," he confirms, his deep voice resonating with finality. He turns to the valley. "There's something else. In the lab a few months ago. My brother was there. His name is Porter, he's my twin. Same height, longer hair. Did you see him?"

I gulp, the icy metal bars that carried Porter's cries fresh as if it were yesterday. Should I tell him?

"Your brother wasn't next to me, but…"

River whips around and hurries over to me. He squats and puts his hand on my shoulder, searching my eyes. "But *what*?"

"He was there."

"How do you know?"

I roll my lips in, cross my hand over my shoulder, and hold my other palm above his wrist.

"Here, let me show you," I touch River's wrist and get a rush of energy. River gasps, and I sense the snapshots of his childhood with Pops flashing through his mind. He startles, taken aback.

"That's quite an ability you have there," River says, a hint of awe in his voice. "When did you first discover you could do that?"

"Since I was a little girl." I run my finger along his warm, calloused palm, and his life and a handful of memories flow through me. "It runs in the family."

I close my eyes, watching young River and Porter playing in the sun in a wheat field. River was a good brother, ensuring Porter avoided trouble. I see him chewing out Porter for almost getting hurt. River cares about people. The images shift to River today, standing alone after they took Porter.

"It wasn't your fault." Tears fill my eyes. "What they did to Porter, losing him. You did everything you could. *Everything*."

He pulls back, but I continue to touch his hand. I trace his palm, reveling in his inner strength. "Porter was in the cage they transferred me to before they moved me. I sensed him when I touched the bars."

He jolts in alarm. "Is he still there? D—Did you see him?"

I shake my head sadly. "No ... echoes of his memories. They killed my sister, Lily. I don't know what happened to Porter, but he wasn't there when they transferred me."

He battles between nodding and fighting back tears, like it's what he'd expected, but it hit him in the gut. He stands and runs his hands through his hair.

"River, wait, I'm sorry, I was trying to help. I..."

He turns his back, his chest rising and falling with labored breaths. I let him have his space.

Grasping his satchel and the near-empty water jug, he steps onto the plateau. He unfurls his wings, avoiding me.

"Where are you going?"

He clears his throat. "I'm going to get some fresh water and food. Try to stay warm and rest up."

"O—okay."

His broad filaments churn the air as he launches skyward. He flies off, and the pain from Dr. Lytle's words echoes in my mind. *"We lost Lily this morning. There were complications. We did what we could. I'm sorry."* Then he acted jovial, whistling his stupid, zippy trademark tune. I was less crass but did the same to River and confirmed his worst fears.

I warm my hands near the fire. *Great job, Delene.*

Chapter Eleven

River

After Pops died, survival became my sole focus—food, shelter, not dying.

I clean the stream water by letting the liquid flow through my fingers and then boiling it, which takes time but is essential. After sealing the container, I retreat to a secluded spot by the stream, far from soldiers' prying eyes. *Steps*.

A rabbit got caught in one of the traps overnight. I clean my knife, washing off the rabbit's blood and leftover meat. I fill the jug with water and pebbles, as Pops taught me. It's a long and arduous process, but the result makes the difference between dysentery and being healthy. *Steps*.

In the back of my mind, I knew Porter was dead. I wanted to believe he wasn't, and somehow, he survived and gave his captors a hard time, being his cheeky self. Concealed, I land on an aspen branch.

I shouldn't be surprised. I did expect this sooner or later, but the reality is ten times worse. I slump against the tree trunk, hugging it, and focus on breathing.

My mind races at night, making sleep elusive. I hate not having closure about Porter. Deep down, I fear he didn't survive, but I hope he's out there, enduring with his wit. If I think about it too hard, grief and sorrow overwhelm me. I can't dwell on them or Porter. Not now.

Scrubbing my hair, I reach for the water jug. The cool liquid soothes my parched throat. I need to focus: check the thicket for traps, find food for Delene, and keep moving. I navigate the slender birches, their peeling trunks resembling skeletal fingers in the gloom. In the silent forest, I listen intently for any signs of life hidden in the undergrowth.

I rouse from my musings, set down the jug, and head into a nearby thicket, scanning the trees.

Near the stream, I stumble upon a nest—still warm—four pale blue eggs inside. The mother is gone, likely finding food. I reach in and take two eggs, leaving the other two. Perhaps the mother bird will try again.

The red-breasted mother swoops, screeching. I shield my eyes, clutching the eggs. "I'm sorry," I call, gliding away. Though it lessens her chances, Delene needs nutrients.

I head back to the bank, grab the water jug, and wrap the eggs in a cloth to protect them from the flight.

With as much as Pops had to deal with, trying to survive, reassess, and raise us, I'm amazed he spent as much time as he did to teach us all he knew. He didn't show affection like you'd expect a parent to. His love came in the form of wisdom and, in detail, valuable things that would come to save my life as he taught me how to trap and snare.

Dreams and shutting my eyes terrify me. Pops was the only one who could calm my fears.

I shouldn't leave the nest, but I need to be alone.

I fly to a beehive in a cliffside nook. It's early, so the bees are still inside. I break off a flat chunk of wood and fly back.

Slowly and carefully, I extract the sticky, dripping honeycomb, fixing the food to the wooden slat. Two bees walk over my hand but barely move, so I've come at the right time.

A buzz comes from the hive. I take off before the bees notice me. I don't often risk bee stings by raiding hives. But I want to make Delene a good breakfast.

I gather wild blueberries, then find solitude to grieve, choking back tears over my brother's death. Though I'd held onto my inner prayers, her confirmation twists my heart. I can't cry in front of her.

Taking my time, I load the slat with dripping golden honey and dewy blueberries, then come across a thatch of wild chicory near the edge of the ridge. I pick six or seven and set them on the end of the slat, yanking them by the roots. The chicory will come in handy. I lay the roots on the slat and scan the area for drones and people.

The tree on which I left the duffel bag is nearby, so I fly there quietly and fix the duffel bag to my chest, securing the straps through my arms. I try to keep the bark slat steady, but there's no way I can fly with this. I hook the duffel bag on a shorter tree branch, where it will be free from predators. I'll come back later. I swipe at my eyes, drier, and fly back to the nest, careful with the food. I present the lavish honeycomb and egg feast, pulse racing in anticipation of her reaction. Delene's eyes widen, her lips parting in an exhilarated "O."

"Mind the honey." I scrape off the wax layer. "There could be bees inside. I took some robin eggs, though the mother might be upset."

"This honey is *wonderful*," she grins, dipping her fingers for another taste. "Amazing. So sweet."

She dives into the blueberries.

"Eat. I'll get firewood." I smile slightly. Porter would tease me for waiting on her hand and foot. People were his department, not mine.

He was the extrovert, while I focused more on an immediate exit and the closest object I could use as a weapon.

I turn toward the cliff, hands in my pockets. Although I've come to grips with my brother's death, Delene's presence still affects me. But it's not as intrusive as I expected. She intuits when I need space, and even though she's injured, she makes herself useful.

"River?"

I turn back. "Yeah?"

"Why are you helping me?"

The question catches me by surprise. Most people wouldn't even ask. If someone's nice enough to lend you a hand, you take whatever they give with thanks. Generosity isn't a huge part of living today. I fiddle with my knife. The blade is clean, but wear shows at the hilt. "I am helping you because ... it's the right thing to do, and Pops would want me to." I can't quite look at her.

"You mentioned Pops. Is he your father?"

"Nah, my grandpa." I look into the distance, a faint smile crossing my lips.

"He told us to do our best with what we have and help others."

Her eyes dance with sunshine. She eats a piece of the honeycomb. "Pops sounds like a good man."

I nod and stare at my feet, where Pops's worn and seasoned boots toe a bit of earth. "He was ... hey, let's boil the eggs and brew coffee from the chicory. Not the real stuff, but it tastes close enough. The soil's good in some areas, and I found a patch growing on the other side of the mountain. When you finish, we can wash the chicory, toast, and mix it with hot water and honey. So, don't eat all the food. Save some for the fake coffee."

"I don't think I could finish it if I tried. Whoa, looks like you ransacked the whole *hive*. There's enough honeycomb here to feed an army." She extends the drizzling slat to me. "Do you want some?"

"Yeah." I crouch, grab a fistful of berries and enough honey to kick my energy up, plus some honeycomb, and have the most excellent breakfast I've had in ages. The sweet tartness of the wild honey with the crisp flavor of blueberries is the most precious thing I've tasted in months.

I'm okay with simple jerky, fish, forest fruit, and herbs, but having someone to care and provide for kicks me into gear in a way I haven't felt in a long time. I like the change. I finish eating and wash my hands, not wanting to gross her out. I check her injury, extending my hand.

Delene hesitates, wary, like she's not sure if she trusts me.

I scoff. "C'mon, would I have gone to the trouble and risk of getting you fresh honey and berries if I planned to hurt you?" I meet her eyes and soften my voice. "I'll be gentle. Trust me."

Her expression shifts, giving me an opening. She draws a deep breath. "Okay, doctor. Let's get this over with."

She extends her wing, and I examine it. *Hmm.* Not as bad as yesterday.

When Porter and I were kids, he fell off a roof when he learned to fly. He sprained his ankle, but we Evol-humans heal quicker. "It's not unsalvageable," I tell her. I glance at her feet, which she's got tucked under her. Blood sprinkles the edges and soles. I take off my pouch and sit on the ground, extending my hand. "Show me your feet."

"That's a bit forward. You haven't even bought me dinner yet." She winces, moves with ginger care, and extends her legs. I lift her left foot, and scrapes and cuts crisscross the underside. It's hard to tell the extent of the damage through the dried blood. I frown.

"This could get infected. Let's clean it and bandage your feet with honey." I snatch my satchel and find the remaining bandages.

I grab a spare white strip of cloth from the ground. It's dirty, but it'll do. I pour water onto the rag and focus on the more severe parts of Delene's feet, where the cuts go the deepest. "How on earth did you climb here without any boots? The rocks alone should have killed you."

"I'm a good climber, I guess." She dips her head like she's embarrassed or something. "My dad taught me."

"Cool," I mutter. I apply honey to her icy feet, wrap each with gauze, and cut the excess with my knife. Then, I sit back on my knees.

"Are you sure a bear won't be licking my toes in the middle of the night?"

I chuckle. Delene's sassy and sweet. "You'll be okay. When it's cold, they keep to the lower ground where there's food and dens." I sit back and double-check the bandage. "That's the best I can do. Keep them on for a day, and we'll check tomorrow."

Chapter Twelve

Delene

As the sun disappears, I snuff the fire. The eight warming rocks will make an excellent heater tonight, a welcome change from the cold chill. River's been gone a while to get something.

The chicory brew tastes like nutty coffee. The raw honey makes it go from bitter to enjoyable. The warmth soothes me as I sip, allowing me to focus on the flavor instead of the pain. The flavor of the honey and fresh blueberries explodes on my taste buds in a burst of sweetness I haven't experienced in years.

I've never tasted raw honey. Visions of bees and plump berries make it even sweeter. How on earth did River get that whole honeycomb out without being stung? I wouldn't go anywhere near a hive. I'm so thankful for the meal. And his kindness. Telling him about his brother was brutal, but he's not mad, which is a relief.

I remove the small comb from the hygiene kit and work through my hair, smoothing the strands. After all I've faced, this stranger helps me, lowering his guard.

There was a spark as he cleaned my wound when I met his eyes, a bond between us. River is different. More than just okay, he's been truly wonderful to me.

From the valley, a blue light beams into the night. Dr. Lytle's visage fills a giant holographic grid. *"Delene Fairborne,"* his voice makes me shiver, so familiar from my caged days. *"I know you hear me. Your vitals from the implanted indicator are on the screen right in front of me."*

My jaw drops. I had no idea Dr. Lytle implanted a biometrics scanner. I search my arms for any sign of an implant, but I find none. I remember a green smoothie pouch they forced me to drink the first night. Did they hide a biometrics chip? That would explain how adamant they were for me to drink it.

Paranoid, I search along my neck, prodding with two fingers for any indication of the chip. Dr. Lytle's voice continues to echo throughout the valley.

"Delene, it's only a matter of time. To the personnel tracking said asset, I will double the reward for the soldier who captures Miss Fairborne alive. Use any means necessary to bring her in, but do not kill her. The soldier who locates her will be abundantly provided for, including your family members, for up to two years if you accomplish this within 24 hours. Double your efforts and bring her in."

I put a hand over my racing heart as River lands on the plateau. "Ah, you put out the fire. Enjoy the light show?"

"Yeah," I reply acerbically. "It's something else."

River lifts an eyebrow and flings a big object onto the air mattress. "Here."

"What's this?" I lift a duffel bag, large but light. The canvas is worn yet still sturdy under my touch. Various hands shuffle through my mind, zipping and unzipping, storing goods inside.

"I looted the bag off the soldiers chasing me. There was a two-way radio in there, which I had to ditch so they couldn't track us, but there were some clothes and toiletries. You might find something useful. I don't know. Check if anything fits so you don't catch hypothermia."

I consider River. His tone sounds rough, like he's been alone for too long, yet his intent is kind. I thank him and unzip the duffel bag. Inside are standard-issue fatigues, a military pullover, thick black socks, and a small hygiene kit with a toothbrush and toothpaste.

I unroll the hygiene kit and giggle. "Wow. They didn't even hook me up this well in the lab. Are you sure you don't want any of this?"

"No, I'm all set." He pats his satchel. "Take what you need."

He lets me use his knife to create slits in the back of the sweater. Slipping into the pullover partially, I set aside my pride and seek his assistance. We get the wings through, and behind the trees, I change into fatigues, adjusting the waist for warmth and fit, a welcome change from my jumpsuit.

I tear fabric for bandages, store them, and brush my teeth. The minty zing awakens my senses and revives the malaise of being injured. I sigh, content. "It's so wonderful I can't describe it."

River chuckles as he passes me.

I set the duffel bag by the containers for protection. Washing my toes to avoid wetting River's bandages, I then dry them and put on thick socks. The warmth is comforting, reminding me how clean, warm feet boost one's mood.

"Better?"

I meet River's eyes. He sits on the other side of the fire pit. "Yes, thanks. My feet are much warmer. It'll help."

"Good. We should, uh, talk about sleeping arrangements." He scratches behind his ear and gestures to the air mattress I sit on. I turn to hide my blush. The last dying embers of the fire crackle as they snuff out for good, sending up wafts of fragrant cedar smoke.

"Sure."

"Last night, I couldn't sleep, so I kept watch, but I'd better get some shut-eye tonight, or I'll be useless come morning."

He stayed up all night so I could sleep? I shake my head, exasperated and torn between appreciation, guilt, and annoyance. "River, you didn't have to do that. I would have—"

"Don't worry. Sleep comes and goes with me. So, we'll take tonight in shifts. I'll take the first two hours, and then we can switch."

"Are you sure? I don't want to inconvenience you."

"Well, too late," he snarks. I purse my lips at his ribbing. "Besides, there's only one blanket, and we should wait until the soldiers leave."

I lie on the air mattress with the scratchy covering pulled to my chin, much warmer with these new clothes. I roll to my uninjured side.

"The blanket's not much, but it'll see us through the night." I sense River's gaze. "You might be cold, though."

"It's fine," I say. "This is a lot better than last night. And hey, I have thick socks. River, thank—"

"Don't thank me yet. Thank me after, when we're both still alive."

I nod, amazed at how my luck has turned. I clawed my way up the mountain the other night, a bare scrap of a person kept for far too long in a cage. And here I am, in a warm outfit, with clean teeth and a full belly. And the best part? I'm not alone.

He wakes me for my shift. I get the sense he let me sleep much longer than he should have because I'm well-rested. River curls on his side and falls asleep in minutes. He's less tense. And handsome. I press my lips together. *Crap.*

Chapter Thirteen

River

When I wake to Delene tending the fire, I instinctively reach for my knife before remembering she's there. I've grown accustomed to being alone.

Over the months, the sounds of nature replaced human interaction so much that it seems weird to have someone here, but I don't mind her company. She's sharp, with a pleasant, throaty voice.

The *rat-a-tat* of gunfire in the distance fills the valley, an echo. Delene shoots to her feet, clutching her wing. "What is that?"

I pinch the bridge of my nose. There's no way I'm going to sleep tonight. I walk to the plateau. "Scare tactics. They used them with me and my brother several months ago. You'd be amazed how many people reveal themselves." I sit near her, take the stick from her hands, and stoke the flames. "Go back to sleep, rest. You won't be any good to anyone without some shut-eye."

"Well, what about you?"

"I'm fine. I had plenty of time to catch some Zs."

Chapter Fourteen

Delene

Awakening to the swish of River's knife sliding back into his sheath, I'm instantly alert.

"I brought hot water," he says, motioning to the bucket. "And some racks to scrub your clothes. Clean up while I'm gone."

I get to my feet, stiff, sore, and sassy. "What, you want me to scrub the place down and polish your boots too?"

"I won't refuse a good boot shine, Princess. Best tidy that wound unless you're aiming for an infection."

I walk to the bucket and dip my hand into the water, relaxing at the sensation. "Mm, *warm*," I moan. Hot water is so rare it might as well be gold. We couldn't light fires at night while on the move, and I was too young to remember when Mom and Dad provided hot water for cleaning.

"I figured freezing stream water wouldn't inspire you."

As I scrub my hands, a comforting sensation spreads through me. The heat soothes my scraped skin, allowing my fingers to flex with less pain. I'm grateful for this minor relief.

"Where'd you get warm water?"

"I have my ways." He says, smug.

"Impressive." I let my eyes linger on River above his muscled shoulder. *Thank you for saving my life, sheltering me, and for your generosity*, I consider telling him, but words fail for what he's done for me. He knows. No one has cared for me this gently since my parents. I'd forgotten the comfort of having someone show concern, even if he's doing it to get me out of his hair. But I don't think he is.

"How are your feet?"

I stand, pleased when the ache is gone. "They don't hurt anymore."

"Good. Maybe we should look."

"Okay." I sit back on the mattress, peel off my socks, and unravel the bandage on my left foot. The skin is pink and healed, with a few bruises at the bottom. I beam at him. "It's so much better. That honey you used did the job."

"I'm glad. Okay, now the other foot." I remove the other sock and bandage, and the skin is healed, with minor redness and tender flesh where the cuts have closed. "It's better." River steps to the plateau. He turns his head to the side, acknowledging me. "Keep the fire burning. It's safe to do in the daylight. Make sure the rocks get warmed and keep the flames and smoke low. If I'm not back by nightfall, extinguish the fire. Wrap the rocks in the bottom of the blanket, and they'll keep your feet warm."

"I will. I promise. Be careful—"

A gust of wind hits me as he swoops from view.

I regard the racks in my hand. Whoever used these last didn't do too good of a job cleaning them. But I have warm water, food, and a generous, grumpy nestmate. I swiftly remove my shirt and get to work cleaning off the grime.

As kids, we once stayed the night in an art gallery, wandering from room to room, taking in murals, sculptures, and portraits. The sky is a portrait stretched on an enormous canvas, a stunning mixture of blue, pink, and purple.

River joins me later as I survey the valley, the scrape of his whetstone sharpening his hunting knife mixing with the cry of hawks nesting in the craggy mountains. "Yep, room with a view. Hard to believe a world this ugly looks so amazing." His eyes linger on me, visible in my side-eye view, while my heart pounds.

"Got any other gadgets stashed away besides that black box up there? A radio or tablet we could use?"

He shakes his head. "No. Pops told me people in the city could track the electromagnetic pulse on some frequency. Do you want to stay safe? Bare essential is the way to do it."

"Show me how the rocks work." My dad taught me a lot about survival, but this is different. River takes cotton balls and kindling from his pouch and puts them in the fire pit. He strikes a match and protects the small fire.

He sits back on his haunches. "Not much to it. Angle the rocks near the flames to absorb heat. Three hours a day, give or take. The longer they heat, the better." He turns to me, serious, and he speaks slowly. "Remember *never* to light the fire at night."

"Do I *look* like I'm stupid? I can survive, doofus. Jeez, I've come this far. I had no idea you could use rocks as a heater."

"Everything I can do came from Pops. They chose him for the trials. Even though he had special abilities, he couldn't fly. He was an airborne Ranger, so he knew about survival."

"He must have been a sharp guy to have raised you." River understands what I mean without me explaining. Back in the day, they locked up candidates like him. For his grandpa to have escaped, he must have been clever.

"He was the smartest man I've ever met." His voice catches, but he covers it up. I understand, having done that once or twice myself. Softness is a dangerous luxury these days. "Here," his voice grows a little harsher. "Come warm your hands."

"Thanks." I edge closer to the low fire, and the flames heat my body and feathers. I sigh and relax. "That's nice."

River clears his throat. "Yeah. I'll check some things and get more firewood. Stay here, keep the flames going, and get warm. I'll be back." He takes two long strides to the plateau's edge and is off.

"A man of many words," I grumble, holding my palms to the fire.

River spends the afternoon teaching me how to prepare bark and make jerky, which is all new to me, but his instructions are clear. After some practice, I'm getting the hang of this. The aroma of smoking meat mingles with the fruity mountain air.

When I use his knife, I shave the bark to what River calls the cambium layer, which is light and thin. He's a patient teacher, River. Despite his stubbornness, I'm surprised by how focused he is when he shows how to slice the bark into thin strips.

"You can eat bark raw," he says, "but it tastes like a shoe. I prefer boiled, like pasta. When I was a kid, I'd pretend boiled bark was spaghetti. I've even mixed in some dandelion greens, which is okay. Not great, but okay. There aren't any dandelions around here, though. Maybe in the spring."

He lets me experiment with the bark while fixing a crossbar rack above the flames. The bland bark would help if we were starving.

He lays each strip over the center rack, leaving a space between them, and shows me how. Knowledge is like currency, and I'm getting *paid*. My family was skilled at fighting and scavenging canned foods from the abandoned military stockpiles that littered the countryside. But River's survival skills are on another level.

River leaves to check his traps below.

Close to sunset, I'm about to store away the strips of bark when River lands, bringing back a wild rabbit. "Dinner." He gets back to work skinning the hide. "I'll teach you how to make jerky." He scrapes the rabbit's hide. "I've got two more traps I need to check, but I've got to be careful. They have drones everywhere. You want to cut the meat up, and I'll be back?"

"Sure."

He sets the fur aside and hands me the meat. When he returns, he hasn't caught any more game, but I've made neat jerky strips.

"Not bad, huh?"

"It's getting there," he muses, eyeing the fruits of my labor. "With more practice, you'll be a pro."

"River ... I want to say I appreciate you teaching me how to do this, and I'll repay you someday."

He points to the jerky on the crossbar with his knife. "Well, you can start by not burning food."

"Oh no," I gasp, dismayed at the sight of the burning strips. But it's too late. The charred sizzle invades my nostrils. I hurry to remove the jerky strips, which are about to turn into coal.

River chuckles. "It's fine. I prefer them crispy anyway."

I drape a fresh strip of meat over the crossbar. "I'm more of an expert at scavenging. What you do is *survive*. Your Pops knew his stuff."

He warms his hands on the other side of the fire, considering the flames with a thoughtful expression. "That he did."

"I can show you other ways to light fires," I offer. I want to do something in return for River letting me stay here. It's saving my life. "I'm also a pro at scavenging cars. There's always something useful, like seat covers, mirrors, and seatbelts for ropes." I turn a strip of jerky over.

"Hmm ... most of the cars in the canyons have already been raided. But I'll fly over the ridge tomorrow and check. May come in handy."

I leave the jerky to smoke, then change my bandage with care. This experience of roughing it, peeling bark from trees, skinning animals, and learning how to create jerky is untapped territory. Given my grandfather's background in special forces and his work in intelligence, he likely knew how to do something similar.

Still, he stuck with the basics and taught us how to rock climb and open a tin can against concrete when scavenging. Maybe he hoped we wouldn't have to fend for ourselves in the wilderness. But scavenging still counts for something. I am good at finding ample food and supplies in a city complex.

My crafty parents knew where to rummage for nonperishable food and a million ways to use an abandoned car for survival. I change the bandage and flip the meat over so the jerky's cooked on both sides. He'd interfere if he thought I did it wrong, but he doesn't, so I suppose I'm learning. I'm torn between appreciation and irritation as River patiently teaches me. Guilt gnaws—his upbringing forced him to learn these talents so young. But he's proven an attentive teacher despite my ineptitude.

As the gristle on the meat smells done, I get ready to remove the jerky. River fiddles with his knife and glances at the meat strips over the crossbar. "Let it cook longer. It should have a leather-like texture."

I examine the withered, wrinkled strips. "Are you sure? They look done to me."

"The meat needs to smoke for well over an hour." River uses the hem of his T-shirt to clean his knife. "To destroy parasites and get the meat at the right temperature. The jerky will last a few months." His wings rest on either side of him. I recognize the motion. Opening and relaxing after a flight is comfortable, like stretching your arms. His feathers shine in the setting sun. I nod and flip the strips over so they get cooked right on both sides.

We fall into a silence.

His wings shimmer, appearing sleek, preened, and healthy.

He's patient, and I like that.

"How are the jerky strips?" River asks a while later.

"I think they're nearly done," I reply. "A bit longer for this side?"

River inspects the strips. "Yep, perfect. Get them off the fire before they burn."

I remove the smoked jerky from the spit.

River grins. "Nice work, high speed. With a bit more practice, you'll be a pro."

I laugh. "I learned from the best."

Labeling River is difficult as he defies easy categorization.

My wound is red, beefy, and tender. I replace the bandage and make sure it's secure. The heat of the water and fire take the edge off.

Beyond the ridge, Dr. Lytle waits. I can't go back. I can't be their guinea pig.

Nature decided to infect humanity, and we happened to be available at the time and have immunity to the plague. If given a choice, I'd save as many people as possible. But they outnumbered us, and I wouldn't let them turn me into a lab rat.

It's nice today, with Utah's patchwork sky of light and shadow. The fire's warmth lifts my spirits. I trace the crude letters of River's name carved into the cliff. How long has he been here? Can we stay undetected?

I clean the dirty rag and let it dry on the rock. I roll my shoulder and try to move my wing, but the joint feels locked and stiff. I would give anything for some medicine to alleviate the pain, but the discomfort at least keeps me alert.

Chapter Fifteen

River

I fly to the stream, focusing on my favorite fish haunt.

I've avoided fishing more than a few times a week because they will give up their territory for a safer location if I trawl too often.

But Delene needs protein and iron if she's going to get well. I catch two large trout and bag them in my pouch. I'll need to scale and debone them first, but coupled with some edible mushrooms and cattails I snag, they'll make a nice meal for us both. Dipping one or two cattails in game fat will also serve as candles. Not that I'm thinking about candlelit dinners or anything.

The path I find is new, barely visible—a line of upturned soil and flattened grass weaving between spindly birch trunks deeper into the forest. It doesn't look like animal trails I'm used to. My fingers graze the rough bark of the trees as I follow silently, senses alert for any sound out of place.

I *could* stay at the nest instead of risking my neck here to get us a fresh game. It's not ideal, but there's at least enough jerky and nuts for a few weeks. But with winter coming, I'm limited in my foraging time before the frost overtakes the land. My stock's only going to take us so far.

Wild carrots grow near the sandier soil where the stream tapers off. I pluck eight purple and red ones. They're ripe, with a few withered. I check them for decay, toss aside spoiled ones, and put the rest in my pouch. I don't want to risk washing them in the stream, so a douse of water at the nest will do.

The grass further inland is wild and undisturbed, and the soldiers haven't been to this area yet. I set a snare near the base of a tree. With any luck, I'll trap some game, and with both of us to feed, we will need more. My brother and I doubled up hunting. We always had supplies. I'll come back later to check on the snares I've set. Near the stream is where the local wildlife seeks water.

I hide the trap with branches and leaves to avoid detection by the soldiers.

Overgrowth hangs on the other side of the tree, and sunlight spills to the forest floor over a random patch of dandelions that have taken over the grass. *Perfect.* I'll clean them off, and we can have them with the fish later.

A nearby twig snaps on the forest floor. I jerk my attention back to the canopy of trees. Something's not right.

I crouch, open my wings, and fly briskly, cloaked in forest shade. I land on a high, bushy pine branch. A fierce soldier emerges, rifle raised, cold calculation in his eyes. He means to kill.

Another soldier catches up to him, eyeing the perimeter. "Anything?"

"No. But I heard something. Might have been the girl."

The second soldier claps a hand to his neck, ending a mosquito's life. "There's nothing here but bugs and trees. She's long gone or dead by now. I'd be shocked if she made it through the night. Wounded and in this cold? The odds ain't good."

The first soldier, the one with death in his eyes, scans around again. These two are a lot sharper than the idiots from earlier, and the last thing I want is to be on the receiving end of a chambered round. I'm well-concealed, but I think the first soldier senses me.

"Maybe," the first soldier grunts. "Let's backtrack and recheck along the riverbank. She can't be far, whether she's dead or not."

"Copy, sergeant."

The sergeant gives one last look, and then they retreat.

A platoon in the distance advances, armed with sleek plasma rifles. Their drones, equipped with tracking darts and tranquilizers strong enough to sedate an elephant, buzz overhead. I wait, knowing their technology far outpaces my bows and blades.

After the soldiers move on, I fly low, scouting the perimeter before returning for water. I collect the few good apples left in a grove near the top branches, but rabbits are still scarce. I hide behind a pine, observing the ruined city walls that taunt me with past horrors. They'd kill us all given the chance. I heft my catch. It's been about an hour—enough time for her to clean.

I spread my wings to leave, then pause. "I'll protect you," I swear. "I *will* protect you." I dive into the wind, returning to her.

Chapter Sixteen

Delene

*The abyss wraps around me, the chilling grip of the lab drawing ever
closer. River's hand slips from mine, and the muffled voices of the
pursuers echo through the mist. Panic rises like bile in my throat.
"River!" I scream, pleading and desperate. I'm not afraid of the lab,
but of losing River, the one constant in my chaotic existence.*

*As they close in on us, River embraces me, touching his forehead to
mine. In a hushed tone, he says, "I won't let them take you."*

My eyelids flutter as I wake. We both fell asleep last night
after a good dinner, surrounded by warming rocks, which have
gone out, but the frost is nothing compared to the memory
of the lab cage against my skin. The power of the high winds
bites with razor-sharp teeth, assaulting the flesh between my
shoulders. I shiver and curl into a fetal position. My feathers are
of no help, as damp and cold as I am.

I tremble until warmth settles around my shoulders and
upper back. I open one eye, and River's right wing drapes across
me. I roll over onto my side, facing him.

"You okay?" he asks gruffly.

"Yeah, just a bad dream. I'm fine."

"What was it about?"

"Nothing," I reply, my voice soft and raspy from sleep. "Just
… something happened to you."

"What, you'd miss me?" he teases. "I figured you'd be glad
to finally get rid of me and have this place all to yourself."

River's dismissiveness and jokey tone ignite my temper.
Does he think this is easy for me? I bite my tongue to quell the
flare of emotion.

As if he senses the shift, River moves closer. His voice is
gentle. "Hey. I'm sorry. Tell me what's going on."

I turn away and wrap my arms around myself, wings tucked in tight. "You don't understand," I rasp. "I can't lose anyone else. When the raiders came, we tried to fight them off, but everything happened so quickly." Tears threaten to spill over as my voice breaks. "First, they cut my mother down. And my father..." A ragged breath shudders through me. "He told us to run while he held them off. Lily pulled me away, but when I glanced back, he fell and got buried beneath them."

River hesitates before laying a hand on my shoulder. I turn back, and his solemn eyes ground me. "I'm sorry, Delene."

I shift closer, taking solace in his steady presence. "You're all I have. If anything happened to you..." I won't insult him by expressing the depths of my fear. He knows.

River tilts my chin up. "Nothing will happen to me. I promise."

I nod and nestle against him. It's enough.

He falls asleep, his breath puffing out visibly, and his nostrils darken in the cold night. His warm feathers envelop me, so I scoot closer instead of waking him. I'm freezing, and he's the only thing preventing me from becoming a popsicle.

His wing curls over me, and he hauls me in close. Jeez, he's strong. I drift into his embrace, enclosed by his shelter. I regulate my breath as I watch him sleep. His mouth is agape, and he's out of it. *Thank God.* I press my ear to his shirt, where his heat radiates into me as his chest rises and falls. Lulled by his wings and heartbeat, I sleep.

Chapter Seventeen

River

Heat surrounds me—a stark change. Delene burrows against me, our feathers mingling. *When did this happen? Why does it feel so right?* I remember her waking from a nightmare. As she sleeps, I study her peaceful, soft features.

Gently, I touch her back. "Hey, wake up."

I half expect a rebuke, but she murmurs, "So warm," pressing even closer.

"Okay," I chuckle. "Tell me when you've had enough of this big chocolate bear."

She rouses, her confusion evident. "What?"

"Ready for the day?" I tease. "Or do you want more cuddling?"

She pulls back, suspicion clouding her eyes. "You cuddled up to *me*. I remember."

I laugh. "*Sure.* However you want to play it. I know what happened."

In mock irritation, she hurls a handful of leaves at me. I pick them off. There's a tense pause where we stand on the precipice of something deeper, but today's not the day. Not yet. I step back, the magnetic pull between us unmistakable.

I hesitate at the plateau and almost speak, but Delene's embarrassed. I give her space—no sense fanning the flames. I'm foolish for even thinking about pursuing this. She'll be gone when she heals anyway.

I sigh and fly to the stream.

"How's the wound?"

Delene glances at her wing. "Good question."

"Let me take a look."

She shifts over, and I inspect the dressing. "I'll recheck it later today. Any better?"

"Kind of." She rotates her shoulder, and her wing gives a slight flutter. "It's stiff." She picks up a slab of bark and gets to work shaving it like she's been here as long as I have.

I stare at her, unsure how to tell her. "River, what—" she begins, her words faltering in alarm.

Scrubbing my hand over the back of my neck, I sit back. "Hear me out. Let's stay together."

She gawks like I've grown a second head. *"What*? What happened to *'I do better on my own,'* and *'I am an alpha male lone wolf?'"*

"I changed my mind." Pops all but nags me over my shoulder. I roll my eyes. "And ... I was wrong," I add, as the phantom nudge pokes harder.

"I'm sorry, I didn't hear you. Say again?"

"I was wrong."

She cups her hand to her ear. "You were *what*?"

I point at her. "Don't push it."

"River, if we're going to work as a team, we can't stay here." Delene continues shaving the bark. "Winter is coming. We'll be buried in the snow if we stay."

I shove my hands in my pockets and assess below. "I agree. But where would we go?"

"Well, what about the ski resorts? There have got to be some in the mountains, right?"

I shake my head. "They were destroyed when the Evol-humans came here and got captured. There's nothing there anymore but crumbles of blown-up concrete and wood chips. That's the first place they would check, anyway."

"Okay. So, what about an island."

"An *island*?" I wave a hand and scoff, returning to her and squatting on the other side of the fire. "Yeah, *right*." I don't hide the skepticism in my voice. I place a fresh log on the fire and poke around until the wood settles and the flames dance. "They'd shoot us five minutes in if we're lucky. But okay, I'll bite. Has this island got a name? Pipe Dream Island? Cloud City?"

She slams the bark to the side and huffs. "What *is* it with you?"

"The world's in ruins, Delene. An island? Be serious."

"Jeez, you're crusty today."

I fold my arms. "It's a long shot, Delene, but we got a good thing going with this place, and if you want me in, I need a lot better than *what if there's an island?*"

"I know it sounds like a gamble, okay? But listen. When the plague hit, human life got infected, and they put everyone on lock down, right?"

"Uh-huh."

"So, what if places like Nantucket, Ellis Island, and Cape Cod remain intact?"

I pause, taking in her words. "There's one way we would know. If we flew there ourselves."

She inclines her head as if to say *precisely*.

"Too dangerous," I say. "We have to lie low."

"If we stay, they'll find us," Delene urges. "You have to trust me here. Dr. Lytle won't stop hunting me. He'll do whatever it takes. I agree we're safe for now, but we *must* move."

"Move where? The junkyard? The swamps? I don't think they'd make a real ideal summer home."

"Have *you* got any better ideas than finding an isolated island somewhere?" She scrapes the bark as I taught her, revealing the edible inner layer. She's an avid learner. "If I manage to fly again, I know we'll find an untouched place. They evacuated enough cities and towns during the war, and I'm sure we can find somewhere. We could stock enough food and supplies."

"*No*. We're done talking about this." I step onto the ledge.

"River," she calls, but I dive off.

Chapter Eighteen

Delene

I cradle my face in my hands.

Stupid.

I can't *believe* I cozied up to River last night. What was I thinking? I run my fingers through my hair and look up.

The sun's higher than in the early morning. I tidy up camp, find a spot to pee, and bury the hole by the tree line, then I braid my hair to the side, tying the end with a spare strip of cloth from what's left of my tattered pants. These new clothes River found are much warmer than those rags.

Pine and wet earth scents drift on the wind. A stream babbles below. Birds twitter in the trees.

I chew on some nuts, then remember to cover the lids. River is an attention-to-detail guy, and I don't want to step on his generosity.

When he returns, he watches me.

River's gaze lingers. I turn away to hide my smile. His woodsy scent carries on the breeze—pretending not to notice grows harder.

Foolish.

The word circulates in my mind, mocking me. Of *course*, River thinks I'm foolish. Why wouldn't he? We thrive in a sustainable green area at eleven thousand feet, providing food, warmth, and camaraderie. I'm talking about taking off without any concrete plan.

I'm not, nor have I ever been, the whimsical type. I do believe we could find other habitable places. If this area sustains life, others will, too. In a contained ecosystem off the main continent, there's probably an area like this one where we will be safe.

I tidy the campsite, picking up trash. The remnants of our stay scattered around serve as a stark contrast to the wild. Each item reminds me of the city's dangers and the need to keep moving. Staying alive has always been my top priority. A bird in the distance flies from the trees into the sky toward the city. Wrong way, my friend.

River probably thinks I've got a screw loose somewhere, but our best chance lies in leaving here and finding an island.

I stoke the flames in the fire. The wood shifts, and a flurry of embers shoots up. I remember the sensation of touching River, the steadiness of his mind.

Touching objects overwhelms me with memories, a barrage of hidden thoughts I usually avoid. But River's mind isn't the chaotic mess I've come to expect from others. With him, there's a solidity—a comforting haven.

His grandfather was harder on him than my parents were on us, but in a caring, responsible way. His Pops ensured he and Porter had everything they needed to become strong men, especially knowledge. It was as if he sensed he wouldn't always be there for them.

The best gift a parent can give a child is not passing along information but helping them become independent and capable.

From his memories, he seems thoughtful, though he might do the whole rough, lone caveman act. It's all smoke and mirrors, because his heart is true, and I trust him.

Chapter Nineteen

River

An island. Yeah, right.

As I wait for fish to bite on my makeshift pole, I scoff, skipping a pebble across the water. We'd make it two minutes, five *tops*. She doesn't want to face the harsh, unforgiving reality we inhabit. Delene doesn't grasp the real world after being in the lab for so long. I know better than to be foolhardy. We can't risk leaving when we're safest here. I'll have to convince her of the danger.

I won't admit this, but I care too much already. Nothing's happening to her on my watch.

A flicker of longing stirs within me at how Delene's hair shines in the sunlight, gold as hay. I stared way too long back at camp. I couldn't help it. She seemed creeped out. I'm always looking for reasons to be near her. She's a rare beauty in this harsh world. She caught me looking at her earlier, and with effort, I wrenched my gaze away. I suck at communication, unlike Porter. He said I needed social skills. But I've always been a lone wolf, not a people pleaser.

People gravitate to confidence, but sometimes, that allure can cover deeper, hidden truths. I found I work better alone.

Delene's a fighter. She has a constant calculation in her eyes: the readiness to flee and justified fear. I've done everything possible to comfort her, keep her warm, and feed her. However, my efforts have their limits, and eventually, she'll want to leave.

Before Delene, survival was mechanical. I drifted on autopilot, numb and practical. Porter's loss gutted me, but I clung to life from sheer habit. Delene's presence changed everything. She awoke feelings long dormant. Now, staying alive means protecting her. I have someone to live for again.

"We stay," I murmur. I catch one fish for our meal. With winter coming, food is scarce. But there's a pull in my gut I've avoided.

I could head to the bunker Porter and I discovered. I doubt Lytle's team knows about it, as they focus more on our blood. The bunker's back wall has lines of military MREs—enough for two at twelve a box for three months. Throw in some tree fruit, and you've got a feast. But I need assistance. I need *her*.

The situation gnaws at me. We desperately need more food for winter, but I can't risk being seen by the soldiers. Torn between providing and protecting Delene, I stash the food and return quietly to the nest. Our survival hangs in the balance.

"Any better?" I remove the pouch and hand it over, avoiding eye contact. Porter would call me stubborn, but I try to prove him wrong and make amends. She unzips the satchel flaps and extracts some fish, which I wrapped in leaves.

"It's okay. I changed the bandage. The skin where the arrow pierced is still healing and tender. In a day or two, I may be able to fly."

"Good."

We don't discuss the island, and I'm nice to her. I avoid staring because I sense it makes her uncomfortable. But I'm hyperaware of Delene's hair, voice, and smell. After so long alone, I've memorized every inch of this nest. I sense when she winces and her little movements while trying to avoid pain. Will medicine do any good?

Maybe we should wait for her to recover over the next few days. We'll need more food to keep us fed, but I don't mind the extra pressure. The absence of Porter left a hole in my life, and while Delene's got me pegged as standoffish, her presence is a comfort. I like having someone to take care of again. It rains toward the evening, and we move the air mattress against the lean-to, then wait out the downpour.

"It's so stunning here," she sighs. "And so easy to forget about how horrible things are."

I ache to touch her, but I nod and observe the rain.

A cry rouses me, not a wounded animal but Delene. Restless, fidgety, she's rolled against me again. "Lily," she whimpers. I stroke her wet cheek. We stayed in the lean-to, the rain continuing overnight. She chokes, sobbing in her sleep.

I breathe her name and pull her in close. Screw my pride. I rest my cheek against hers, offering what comfort I can. Her cheek is wet from her tears, soft. Her hand slides into mine, and she laces our fingers together as she nestles back into me.

I exhale and close my eyes as she quiets, soft and warm against me. I've never kissed a girl before, impulsively pressing my lips to her silky hair. I pull back, pulse racing. She relaxes into my embrace, and her breath evens out in the steadiness of sleep.

Awake and captivated, the powerful presence of her nearness holds me. My mind wanders to the last time I was this comfortable and warm, which I can't recall, at least not in this way. Delene makes a slight noise as she burrows deeper into my shoulder. She sighs, and I let my smile surface as she sleeps quietly.

I kiss her forehead. She nuzzles in, content.

What does she dream about? She's petite with delicate features, the kind you'd expect from a fairy tale picture book of the princess. But she's no princess—she's a warrior. I clench my fists, thinking of how they justify harvesting us as if they have the right to live more than we do simply because we're different.

Pops mentioned a long time ago, they kept people apart because of the color of their skin, like having different bathrooms and stuff. It's as absurd as saying the sun shouldn't rise with the moon in the same sky. Makes no sense, right?

Sometimes, late at night, I wonder—if hatred hadn't divided us, could we have avoided this broken world? Would we still have the same outcome? Hard to tell. But if more racist issues had piled onto today's problems, I might never have met Delene.

And that thought scares me.

I maneuver to get more comfortable without disturbing her, and she gently sighs. After a lifetime of running, even if this is foolhardy or a figment of my imagination, I finally have someone worth protecting.

Chapter Twenty

Delene

He steps past, securing his satchel. "C'mon."

"One wing out, remember?"

He sighs dramatically. "Make *me* do all the work."

River lifts me effortlessly, his solid muscles reminding me of movie heroes rescuing damsels. His warmth is heavenly, but I school my expression. No *way* am I going to blush.

He adjusts his hold. "Comfy?"

I catch River's smirk. Yeah, alright. If Lily were here, she'd be thrilled.

"You might want to hold on," he advises.

I wrap my arms around his neck, and my feathers graze him, eliciting a shiver. "Where are we going?"

"It's a surprise. Hang on," River mutters.

Held close to his warm chest, my shivers don't go unnoticed. Suddenly, we're airborne. The sharp mountain wind tugs my hair as passing clouds chill our skin. I cling to River, comforted by his embrace. Cradled close, I feel safe and cherished.

This is true freedom.

River flies steady and accelerated, and I grin. He locks his arms around me and takes us to the trees, dodging swiftly in and out of shadowy pockets.

Held securely in River's grasp, we rise above the Wasatch Mountains. The wind sweeps past, caressing with cool fingers. Below us, jagged peaks emerge from a vast sea of clouds, and the valleys unfold like tapestries. Sunlight dances, transforming meandering rivers into ribbons of liquid silver. Everything is boundless and pure from this height, with the world sprawling beneath.

I haven't smiled in so long that the movement is unfamiliar, wax-like, as the corners of my lips twitch. The sun proves an excellent, delightful medicine. River flies swiftly. Brambles and trees rush past in a blur as he lands us near the mouth of a cave hidden deep in the forest.

The narrow, blade-like cave opening resembles a worn attic closet door, allowing one person through at a time.

River sets me on my feet, and I turn to him.

"Where are we?"

He puts his finger to his lips, tossing his head to the forest. I nod. Others might be close.

He moves past me, and I follow him inside the cave entrance. I tuck my injured wing in, careful not to scrape the rock.

"I found this hot spring while I hid from the searchers," River says. I skirt around the confined space, expecting pitch-black. A gap in the cave ceiling casts rosy light over a shimmery purple lagoon.

"Cool," I reply, my voice echoing off the cave walls.

I don't smell sulfur, just water. I slip off my socks, walk to the pool's edge, and dip my toe in. The water's warm, not too hot or cool.

"I'll wait outside," he says, avoiding my eyes. "If you want to clean."

I smirk. "Tired of my stench? I don't blame you. It must be tough living with someone this stinky."

He ducks his head. "Right. Do you need my help getting in, or can you manage?"

I scoop water into my hand, the warmth relaxing my shoulders. "How deep?"

"About three feet. Shallow. You'll stand."

"Okay." I glance over my shoulder. "Thanks. I'll call if I need you."

"Don't strain your wound." In typical River fashion, he grunts and leaves the cave without another word. I've never worried about him being creepy, unlike Cameron. He's respectful and a gentleman, which I like. Even if he fusses and dotes.

His protectiveness does things to me.

I remove my clothes. River's not the most talkative guy on the planet, and he's the strong, silent type. I could be stuck with a total blabbermouth jerk, which would drive me batty.

I immerse in the balmy water, delicately preening each feather of dirt. The motions soothe and remind me of childhood when grooming my feathers was my only concern as Lily chattered about her latest crush.

The water falls from my feathertips, creating ripples in the light. Each stroke and pull returns me to normal. Clean feathers boost my strength and confidence.

I haven't enjoyed a proper shower in months and never bathed, even as a child. We used a faulty solar-heated shower in the bunker that lasted two minutes. They sprayed me with glacial water in the lab to punish my stubbornness.

I smile. This, *this* is heaven.

I emerge from my bath, reborn, ready to take on the challenges of this world with River by my side.

"You good?" River leans against the cave, knife ready.

"Yes, thank you."

"How's your wing?"

"It's okay. It's better than it was."

"Good. We should get back."

He moves to pick me up. I gesture for him to wait. "Let me try something."

I turn my back to him and slowly untie the blood-crusted field dressing, wincing as the fibers peel away from tender flesh. The scrap flutters to the ground, and I stretch.

His eyes scrutinize me. "Don't aggravate your injury. How do you feel?"

I breathe deeply. "Sore, but I can move." I test my injured wing. Pain follows.

River reties my bandage as he scolds me. We may heal fast, but my wound still needs time.

I let River carry me again as if he's walking me through a bridal threshold or something, and then we're off. He takes a different route than the one he took last time, circling the mountain and staying hidden. The temperature drops by at least ten degrees the higher we go, and then we're back at the nest.

I thought River was a jerk, but he keeps surprising me. He sets me down with delicacy. Our eyes flit over each other's as he walks to the fire.

Later, while River's off on another errand, I drape jerky strips over the crossbar above the low fire, close enough to smoke but far enough away not to burn. The stones near the flames heat my toes from a foot out. I peel off the socks and let them heat on a rock so they'll be warm tonight.

This raw wilderness thing is something my parents never knew how to do. I'm grateful River's here.

My grandfather was on the first team of the original Evol-human test subjects. He worked in Navy intel and died before I came into the world, so I never got a chance to meet him. The recruits wanted to propel humankind forward, not cause chaos and bloodshed.

What would the initial recruits think of this? The bedlam, the hunting of us, the blood and organ harvesting. It's unsettling such unrest comes from a simple desire for progress.

Wings flap in the wind, and I turn north, where River flies toward me. His satchel bulges at his waist. Did he get food? He lands on the plateau, and a strange fondness strikes me. He can be crusty and cranky, but the truth is, I'm thankful he's around.

"River." I raise the binoculars, my eyes trained on the speck. I repeat his name. He's busy getting the fish he caught earlier.

"What?"

"C'mere."

He joins me, and I point at the shiny object off in the distance. I hand him the binoculars. "There, on the other side of the stream."

He adjusts the binoculars, focusing where I point. "What, the Jeep?"

"Yeah." I shrug as if to say, *Isn't it obvious*?

River hands me the binoculars back. "And?"

"There's no one there. The Jeep has a rearview mirror." I follow him back to the fire and sit on the opposite side.

"What's your point?"

"The mirror. If we could swipe, grab, and go, the reflection would be perfect for fires once the matches are gone. They might also have left a couple of MREs in the back of the Jeep."

He continues to clean the fish and cut the meat cagily. "That's dangerous."

"Yeah, but think about it. The soldiers wouldn't even know we were there."

"You're not a hundred percent on flying yet."

"You're right, but we may not get another chance like this."

He passes me the knife and fish and holds his palm out. "Let me see the binoculars again." I hand them to him, and he walks to the plateau, spying on the Jeep. "If I'm going to go, I've got to go."

"Okay ... please be careful. I'll cook the fish."

"Sounds like a plan." He lowers the binoculars and swoops away. He's good at going through trees quietly. Lily always flew loud, chattering and bumping branches. She had an alluring smile that melted everything in sight. A twinge of emotion hits me as I picture her cheerful smile and hear her bubbly laughter. When we were younger and unaware of the world's complexities, we smiled while playing as our parents decided on our survival plan. How unassuming we were then, simply taking life as it came.

Distracted watching River, I forget the cooking fish. Two clicks from the Jeep, he's clear, rocketing to tear off the rearview mirror in seconds. They should scan the forest floor rather than the trees.

"Nice," I mutter. My eyes linger on the solid curve of River's shoulder and the powerful span of his sleek plumage. "Eyes on the prize, Delene."

River pokes his head over the seat and grabs something, but I can't tell what from this far away. A movement catches my eye. I shift the binoculars left and curse.

Dr. Lytle's soldiers round the bend, heading straight for him. "River, get *out*," I shout helplessly. He's still searching, unaware of how close the convoy is.

River's head jerks up. Bug-eyed, he scans left and right. Clutching his findings, he shoots away as the convoy turns.

"Get out," I chant.

He disappears into the trees. I sigh, relieved, and train my gaze on the convoy.

The first Jeep stops, and the soldier in the passenger's seat stands as he scans the area shrewdly. He barks at the driver and sits, tense. *Did he spot River?*

I recheck the tree line. River's nowhere in sight. Good. He's stealthy, and he can get back okay with a bit of luck. I don't wait long.

Less than an hour later, River flies over, winded.

"Hey," I pass him the bottle of water. He pants and drinks. "Was it worth it?"

He sets the bottle on the ground and unzips his satchel. He removes the rearview mirror and passes me the prize and a large tan packet. He also holds a small, closed black pouch. "For a mirror, an MRE, and a hand saw? *Oh* yeah."

I whoop for joy.

I lie awake, gazing at the stars, the memory of us sharing the fish and MRE still fresh. Ah, contentment, a sensation I've missed. River's presence amplifies my peace.

Lily and I promised each other—to stay focused and avoid boys. The rules seem less clear as I look at River, who's sleeping with his arm over his head and lips parted. The contrast of our skin tones, his smooth dark against my light, creates a mesmerizing caramel blend whenever we touch. I can't help but admire him, especially his lips. I turn away, cheeks flushed.

What am I doing?

I don't know, but as strong as my instincts are to survive, I sure have let my guard down, which I don't do for anyone.

I slip the knot off my field dressing and smooth my hand over the wound, checking. I smile. My feet are better, and the wing's almost healed. I check the exit gash on the other side. The bump is tender, but the skin healed and scabbed. I stand, extend, and give a slight, slow flutter.

It's still sore, but I believe I should be able to fly as soon as tomorrow.

After everything River did for me, could I abandon him? The thought of inconveniencing him pains me. He's not the chattiest guy, and boy, is he moody, but I like him more than I care to admit.

River is stubborn in his ways but genuinely good-hearted. He looks out for me without being obliged to. My dad always said integrity is vital. River has that in spades. I leave the strips of cloth on the ground and return to the air mattress. I'm quiet when I lift the blanket and cozy up to River, the movement second nature. He shifts against me and settles his arm around me.

He must be awake. Compelled, I trace his face. I will try to fly tomorrow. His stubbled jaw is coarse, his cheeks smooth and warm. He stutters a breath below me. I withdraw my hand and tuck it into my chest. I'm warm and safe. River's heartbeat intensifies.

I concentrate on my breathing until his racing heart slows. I nestle my forehead into the crook of his neck. His wings curl around mine, and my hand relaxes against his chest as I drift off. Yes, tomorrow.

"When would you want to leave?"

River passes me two strips of jerky and a handful of nuts. We sit on the edge of the plateau at midday. He didn't say a word when we woke tangled like a pile of puppies in the silver-blue morning light to a sparse dusting of snow. River took the brunt of it, shielding us both from the cold and wet. A light mantle drapes over the pines, accentuating the branches.

The ground at our feet is dusted white on waking, but I'm warm in River's arms, and he has the good grace to roll over and let me get up first. He shakes the snow from his feathers closer to the cliff and is nice enough not to mention the drool patch I left on his shirt.

The snow's cleared, and I take a small bite as we sit. "Today, if possible." I search the skies. The snow has stopped, leaving an overcast gray sky hinting at a brewing storm. "It's only a matter of time. The heavy snow will hit, so the sooner we leave, the better."

We. I'd intended to tell River I would go today. Still, the word *"we"* had other plans, namely River, and I asked if he wanted to leave with me before I knew what had happened.

He eyes my wings. "Think those wings are up for a test flight yet?"

"One way to find out." I set my food on the rock and stand.

"Careful. Don't tear it open."

I nod and flap twice. The wound healed even more overnight. My feet lift off the ground, and I hover in midair, testing.

"Are you in pain?"

"No, I'm ... fine." I check for blood, but nothing. The wound sealed where the skin grew over. I fly higher, then come back. "I think I'm good."

River's eyes scan me, and he stands, concerned. "Are you sure leaving is the right move? We could build a cabin here with the hand saw and use car hoods for a lean-to. We *could* make it here."

"With what, warming rocks and one thin outfit each? We'd freeze to death, River, and you know it."

"We've done okay so far." He sighs. "Why do you want to leave so badly? We're safe here."

"For how long?"

He returns to the fire, blowing on the embers to rekindle the flames. "There's nowhere else. Not for our kind."

"Lily thought me crazy, but they want to clone us. It's why they test and keep us. Dr. Lytle turned nasty when I refused tissue samples. I overheard him and another doctor discuss cloning us for blood harvesting."

River's eyebrows shoot up. "Did they?"

I shake my head. "They might have, I don't know. They can barely find any of us to draw from, and the lab has supply shortages. Their equipment isn't in the best shape, so it's news if they pulled cloning off. Dr. Lytle wants to."

"Do you know what they did to Lily?"

"No, not everything." I fold my arms around my knees and bring them into my chest. "And to be honest, I don't want to know. River, I care about humanity, and if I could donate blood to help a few people live, of course, I would. But what they're doing at the lab is unforgivable. It's inhuman, and I will never forgive them for taking Lily."

Chapter Twenty-One

River

I give Delene some space and busy myself around the nest. I check my gear, seal the food containers, and reinflate the air mattress. The blanket of cloud cover tucks the nest in the gloom, concealing everything but pines from view. It's the perfect place to hide or light a fire on days like this. The height is an optical illusion from a distance, like a cluster of mini forests with no room for human habitat. I almost passed the opportunity to stay here. Luckily, I flew over again and noticed the plateau near the cliff—a blink-and-you'll-miss-it spot.

A day will come when we must leave. Part of me knows this: as you know snow is inevitable in winter. I guess I'm holding on, as always, to an extra day and a spare slice of freedom for us both. It does get cold, and an average human would freeze to death at this altitude if they stayed as long as I have. Our bodies will adapt, and we have the warming rocks. And each other.

I let my gaze linger on Delene and then peer at the pine trees dotting the distant mountains, etched with white and silver, matching the snow beneath our feet. Snow poses a challenge, but I can construct a small log shelter. After all, if I can make a solid raft, lashing and insulating a cabin won't be much different.

As the sun dips below the mountains, the last dying rays set the snow aglow in orange and pink. I place a small pot filled with fresh powder over the crackling fire. Rubbing my palms together, I hold them out to absorb the warmth. I clear my throat. "Tell me about how you came to be on your own," I ask Delene, my voice husky from the chill.

She shifts, tucking her legs beneath and to the side as she pokes the fire. "Uh, we had our parents, but they died when they raided our hideout last year. Then it was me and Lily. They captured and took her away. I lasted about a week when they caught me living off canned goods and what I could scavenge. They told me she died, and I escaped a week later." She sighs, taking on the mien of someone much older and weathered. "So here I am, on the run but alive. And I have no one."

"That's not true." The words escape my lips before I let them. The wind blows my feathers from behind, almost like Pops is here, practically breathing down my neck and kicking me up the backside to offer this girl comfort. I bet he looked at the pearly gates, told them heaven was a "No-Go," and decided he had to stalk me in the afterlife as if I didn't have enough problems to worry about.

I step forward and crouch near Delene, closer than I would with anyone else. "You have *me* if you want me."

She blinks like she's trying to decide whether I'm serious.

There's only one way to show her.

I cup her cheek and search her deep blue eyes, a lovely shade of violet in the gloom. When I'm sure she won't object, I lean in and kiss her. Her lips are soft and warm against mine. I could kiss Delene all day.

She relaxes, clutching my shirt to pull me closer. I encircle her with my arms and lean in for more. I'm exactly where I want to be.

After a while, we reach an endpoint, and I touch my forehead to hers when we break apart. The tension dissolves, replaced with something comfortable and familiar.

"I do want you," she utters softly.

"Good thing, because you're stuck with me," I quip back, unable to keep a straight face.

We laugh like idiots. I take one look at her lips and dive in for another kiss. A gust pushes me closer, and I smile into the kiss.

All right, Pops, I get the hint.

Kissing Delene is like Christmas. Our differences don't matter. When someone's soul touches yours, it moves you. Pops used to say that prejudice comes from misguided thoughts and fear of the unknown. Being an Evol-human is the same. I hold Delene close, pressing my chin into her hair. I need this. I need *her*.

To my surprise, Delene snuggles closer, hands trailing along my arms. I like the stark contrast of our skin tones, a rugged blend that stands out, like us. I guess she does, too, because she cuddles close. I hold her for a while, thankful for having someone who cares about me as much as I care about them. I've never had this with anyone.

Chapter Twenty-Two

Delene

Though I often mocked Lily's romantic notions, in River's arms, I understand there's more. He gets me, cares for me, keeps me safe. I want to stop running, stay with him, hold him close, and replace scary memories with better ones. Maybe we can. I soften and smile up at River.

He quirks his mouth to the side, amused. He seems on the verge of teasing me, but his face falls as he focuses on something behind me. I frown and sit up.

"River? What—"

"Get *down*." He pushes me to the ground. Before I turn, the furious flutter of his wings grazes mine as he launches into the air. A bullet whooshes past me, less than an inch away from my ear. I scream and cover my head.

I turn, and River is in the air, trying to dismantle the drone. I gulp. It's over. As he struggles, spinning midair with the drone, I hurriedly stuff fistfuls of food and bundles of musty blankets into the worn duffel bag.

I grab the bag and fly as River yanks the drone, which crashes over the cliff.

I hold up the duffel bag. "I've got some stuff. Let's go—"

"Delene, *look out*."

But it's too late—a crossbow arrow pierces my thigh, its purple tassel waving. An instant later, a heavy net drops, ensnares me, and flips me upside down. I struggle in midair to break free as something mechanical carries me away.

A drugging sensation fills my body. I sway. I'll be down for the count in a matter of seconds.

River appears, beating his powerful wings as he desperately saws at the net with his hunting knife, the worn handle slick with sweat in his grip. But the net is made of a lightweight super-polymer we call FlexFiber, more potent than steel—developed by military scientists to trap renegade Evol-humans like me. He fights relentlessly to stay close, his mighty wings flapping futilely as the mechanical net drags me away. I run my hand over part of the net. I attempt to speak, but my tongue is heavy as marble.

"River. *River.*" He doesn't hear me, hacking away. I yell his name. "Stop. You won't be able to cut it. Go, there will be more drones. Hide. Hide in the cave."

"Not on your *life*," he growls. I cover his hand with mine and pour my heart through my eyes. A heaviness hits me, a sluggish sensation like I haven't slept in weeks.

"River, go. They can't capture you, too."

The whorl of an oncoming drone catches our attention, and we both glance to the left. River swears under his breath and shoots me a pained expression. As the drone drags me away, I finally meet River's anguished eyes. "I love you," I mouth silently.

The darkness swallows me.

Chapter Twenty-Three

River

They took her.

I desperately search the skies. My heart pounds, my thoughts racing. Where is she? What if ... No. I can't think like that. Crying won't help her. I have to stay strong.

As the last fiery rays disappear behind the western ridges, I emerge from the cave, unfurl my wings, and fly east as the first evening stars appear. I soar over the dark valley, bitterly cold wind slashing my cheeks, headed toward the glow on the horizon—the ruins of Salt Lake City. My wings make evading the drones and sensors at night more manageable.

I don't rationalize or even stop to think. I fly. I fly at a supersonic pace, with nothing but Delene on my mind.

This mission is suicide, but I must try—Delene's worth fighting for.

I soar above the city, the weight of decay and abandonment evident like mold on rotted fruit. Flowering vines wrap around aged brick walls, reclaiming the city—relics of the past rise around me—skeletal high-rises with windows like vacant eyes. Jagged chunks are missing from some structures, and the glass and steel bones are picked clean.

Weeds and vines choke the cracked pavements and streets like nature's virus. Time stains, graffiti slogans, and gang symbols in neon colors mark the crumbling brick walls. Empty windows gape like missing teeth in abandoned buildings. Hollowed ruins of rusted cars sit jacked up on stacks of bricks.

Water-filled potholes reflect the overcast sky, creating a mirror-like effect as I fly over. Tainted with oil, a sluggish creek, filled with debris, winds its way.

Searching for hope here is fruitless. Does compassion remain when the world turns cruel? Or do we become animals when facing death?

I keep flying, looking for the lab.

I glance down, and my heart freefalls like a stone through my stomach. Amid the decay, past the flickering trash fires in alleys and figures huddled around them are clusters of people—or what's left of them. They scatter around, their clothes tattered, moving with desperate urgency. Some scavenge, turning over debris, maybe hoping to find something edible or usable. Others cling to each other. Their scrappiness tells stories of hunger, fear, and loss—all those months of self-pity in the mountains pale to this.

The city streets below present a wasteland—cracked pavement, faded graffiti, and overturned rusted cars. Desperate people in tattered clothes search dumpsters and scavenge. Trash fires throw shadows. Near a crumbling downtown pharmacy, a frail man clutches a limp child. A girl about my age sifts through debris, her arms covered in grime. Even after all I've faced, the devastation overwhelms me. When you think about how hard your life is, all you need to do is witness someone else's struggle to put things into perspective.

Everything is raw and immediate. Even for a guy like me, it's hard to take in.

The wind strikes my face, sharp and cold. I smell burning plastic and paint from the trash fires mixed with the decay's sweet stench. I don't fly straight in. I stop, hide behind trees and buildings, and observe. I have to act wisely.

I spot my destination. I fly over the high wall and descend onto an unlit roof. The lab lights sparkle several hundred feet away. I search below for a way in. They're letting military trucks through the gate. But I can't simply hop onto the back and cruise on through.

I swoop through an abandoned alleyway, careful to land softly. The garbage bins on either side of me reek of rotten sewage. Jeez, I miss the mountains already. I wrinkle my nose at the sharp tang of smoke, chemicals, and pollution clouding the air.

I peek around the corner. The supply truck is near the entrance. A security soldier speaks with the driver. Both wear protective masks. They stand at the end of the truck, with the back door slightly ajar. The soldier signs something on an electronic device and speaks to the driver. He motions for the driver to follow him, and they walk around to the driver's side.

Seeing no threats, I fly to the truck and sneak inside, hiding behind boxes aided by a thin stream of light. A minute later, the doors slam. I gulp.

I don't want to do this, but I can't let Delene die.

Chapter Twenty-Four

Delene

A sharp ring hits my ears as I wake. I'm upside down, bright LED lights washing out the room's color. Chemicals burn my nose, but I can't hide a nauseating undertone.

I look around and see another Evol-human hanging like me. His wings catch the light, their edges blurred. "River?" My voice is a whisper.

The lab's intense light, sharp tools, and flickering fluorescents immerse me in cold fear. The Evol-human dangles beside me, tubes inserted cruelly. His eyes close in agony.

Images crash into my mind: his capture, eyes widening in fear, a needle's bite. Sympathy surges in me. I first think it's River, but then realize it's Porter, his twin, his mirror image. We need to collaborate if we're going to flee this hell.

Something pricks my arm. I see a needle drawing my blood, with a strong bleach smell trying to hide darker scents. "I'd ask where I am..."

"As sharp as ever, Delene." Dr. Lytle taps his pen, ankle crossed. I blink, trying to stay steady as a rush of dizziness comes over me.

"Hey."

"Allow me to introduce you to River's brother," Dr. Lytle says, beaming. "Porter Shaw, this is Delene Fairborne, the miscreant giving us the runaround while you generously supplied vast amounts of your precious blood." Dr. Lytle's chair legs scrape across the linoleum as he leaves his desk. A soft swish of fabric moves past my right ear, and he stands before me.

"Well, aren't you going to say hello to your neighbor, Delene?"

"Go drain *your* blood, you demon," I snarl.

He tsks. "Oh dear. All your time spent in the wilderness did nothing for your manners. I'll leave you two to get acquainted while I rustle up some dinner. Why don't you hang tight there for a while, hmm?" He saunters off, whistling his happy melody.

I turn my head to Porter. "Porter? River will be thrilled when he finds out you're alive."

"Awesome. I *live* for his reactions," he rasps, his voice scratchy. "You know him?"

"I do. We met in the mountains. River thought you were dead. I'm so glad you're all right."

Porter coughs. "Not for much longer. I'm a shell at this point. They've taken every drop I have. Hey, if you get out of here, do me a favor and tell River I—"

"No," I snap. "Save it and tell him yourself."

He laughs. "You're stubborn."

"One of the effects of spending time with River."

"Yup, you know him."

"Look, hold on, okay? I'm getting us out."

"Not going to be a problem. I'll hang around and look at some more medical equipment."

My hands tingle below me, clasped at the wrist with electronic cuffs. I lift my head and survey the room. They brought me here when they took my blood. There's a guarded door in the center of the opposite wall, where we could escape.

"What are you thinking?" Porter asks.

I glance at him. "If I get Dr. Lytle to touch me, I might be able to get a key or somehow get loose. I have firsthand knowledge of what scares him."

"You've got heart, I'll give you that. But let's get real. The quacks have been doing this to me for who knows how long. They'll siphon us like a crop field, take the last bit of our blood, get us well again, rinse, and repeat. It's straight-up torture."

"Delene *Fairborne*." The soft, deep voice I came to dread during my imprisonment, Cameron, surprises me. He crept in while I spoke to Porter and stands facing me, the polish on his black boots shining like diamonds.

"Hi, Cameron," I reply, adopting a gentle tone despite my inner need to vomit at the sight of him.

He grunts, tugs his trouser legs to get more comfortable, and squats close. He shakes his head, looking genuinely sorry. "Oh, Delene. I never wanted this to happen to you."

"Then why don't you release my ankle cuffs and help us?"

He rubs his palms together and quirks his mouth to the side. "I can't do that."

"Sure, you can," I say. "Five tiny minutes, our little secret."

"Let me guess. You'll make it *worth my while*? Like last time?"

"I was ju—*ow*." He grabs my chin in his hand, squeezing hard.

"Hey," Porter shouts, thrashing against his restraints. "Knock it off, man."

"They beat me until I couldn't *stand* for letting you escape," Cameron snarls. The maliciousness in his voice sends an icy blast of fear through me. He has always been crazy, no matter how nice he might have been to me. "Is there anything you'd like to say here?"

"They killed my sister," I breathe.

He releases my chin with a growl and straightens, standing. "You're a stupid, stupid, pretty girl. You've played all your cards. This is on you." He huffs, then walks off.

Tears blur my vision. From the corner of my eye, Porter watches. "Charming guy."

"Oh, he's great. He'd be a real sweetheart if he weren't missing basic human emotions, social cues, and *sanity*."

"You called it."

"Porter?" He meets my eyes. His skin is sallow and a much lighter brown than River's silkier, darker hue from blood loss. "I swear to you, we *are* getting out."

Chapter Twenty-Five

River

At nine, Pops spent days teaching us escape tactics. At fifteen, we trained in hand-to-hand combat and fighting. He ensured we could defend ourselves and each other. His lessons saved our lives.

Pops told me he wished he'd spent the same time with my father, and if he had, Dad might be alive. I don't know. It's a harsh world. Chances are, something might have happened, anyway. Nothing's sure. But I'm grateful my grandfather cared.

So, when the medical attendant comes into the back of the truck to get a box of supplies, I waste no time. My instincts scream to run, but I force myself to stay hidden amidst the boxes. The medic has made his choice to work for a monster. That doesn't absolve me of responsibility for my actions. But I'd do anything to save Delene, even this.

I swoop, knock him unconscious, and take his coat to stay concealed. I drape his ID lanyard over my neck and swipe a baseball cap and tablet from a table near the door. I fix the hat low over my forehead. My wings are massive, and my feathers peek out from under the lab coat, but it's better than strutting in there like a peacock on display. They won't notice if I act like I know where I'm going. *Great plan, genius.*

"Hey," a man calls up, "you done in there?"

"Yep," I mutter, pulling the door shut. I march past, head low. "It's all yours." His eyes drill into my skull, but I can't look back.

The guard buzzes me in. I walk purposefully, glued to the clipboard. In truth, I have no idea where I'm even going. Delene could be anywhere: the bottom floor, the top.

I stroll through a long hall as if minding my business. It's weird to be in an actual building after so long in the wilderness. The regulated air is stale, and the fluorescent lighting seems unnatural and oppressive. Two armed soldiers stand at parade rest, guarding a set of double doors labeled Restricted Area. Not allowing my eyes to linger, I march past and dart into the bathrooms on the left.

I check the urinals and stalls, but the bathroom appears empty. I breathe deeply and splash some water on my face from the sink. I stare at my reflection, half-hidden beneath the baseball cap. I focus, hardening my eyes. "Okay ... think. *Think—*"

The bathroom door creaks and I make a beeline for the accessible stall, rushing in. I lock the stall door behind me and go back to the wall. I trip on the floor and bump into it with a loud thud.

Crap.

A rather musical whistle echoes in the bathroom, then stops as I bang into the wall. "Whoa. You all right in there, buddy?"

I clear my throat. "Mmhmm."

"Okay, then." The man's melodic voice breaks into a deep chuckle. "I guess when you gotta go, you gotta go." He continues whistling. I lean my head back against the wall.

Come on, man, wash your hands and walk away.

Water runs at the sink, echoing around the room.

"Got to get this nasty Evol-human blood off. You know?"

I grunt and make a noncommittal noise, though my stomach sours at what his words imply.

"Say, are you new here? Don't think I've heard your voice. And I'm good with voices."

I deepen my tone. "No, I'm usually on the night shift. I'm helping since someone called in sick. We're bringing in supplies."

"Oh, you work graves. You must know Kenny."

I pinch the bridge of my nose. Who in the world is Kenny?

"Yep. You know him, too?"

The man laughs. "Sure do. I love the guy. Good old Kenny."

"Mmhmm. Good old *Kenny*."

"I'm Dr. Martin Lytle. Marty, to my friends." The faucet turns off, and ice water fills my veins. "I didn't catch your name, friend."

Rage consumes me. I peer out the stall's crack, but the row of stalls blocks my view of the sinks. This man murdered my brother. While my primary mission is to rescue Delene, I won't let this opportunity to avenge Porter's death slip away. I remove the disguise and fly to the top of the stall in a silent, swift move.

I crouch on the edge of the stall door, bracing my hands and feet. I spy the top of Dr. Lytle's silver head near the mirror.

Dr. Lytle takes two steps back and comes into view, and his cunning eyes widen in surprise. For all his murderous tendencies, he seems friendly. I shake my head in disbelief.

"You don't need my name. You'll know my fury."

I slam into Dr. Lytle, white-hot wrath coursing through my veins.

We crash into the sinks in a tangle of limbs, the porcelain cracking under our weight. I punch his nose. Cartilage crumples under my knuckles.

Lytle screeches like a feral cat, clawing at my eyes with jagged fingernails. I knock his hand away and drive my knee up into his gut. He doubles over with a tortured grunt but recovers swiftly, clutching my throat with viselike strength. Fiery pain—my windpipe narrows. Gasping, I knock my elbow into Lytle's ribcage. A bone gives way with a crisp crunch, like a twig beneath my boot. He howls and releases his grip.

I whirl around and grab his hair, smashing his cheek into the mirror. Fear flickers through his cruel facade in the reflection as he confronts his mortality. He's afraid. Then, a spiderweb of cracks erupts in the glass. I snarl and throw Lytle to the hard tile floor, where he writhes, blood slickening. But hatred still burns in his eyes. I raise my boot, prepared to extinguish the life from him, but murder isn't what I'm here for. I land a hard punch to his face, then stop when he passes out.

"Delene."

I remove his key card and drag him by the ankles into the accessible stall. I lock the stall door and fly over it. It's time to get Delene.

Chapter Twenty-Six

Delene

"I changed my mind."

I open my eyes and quickly close them against the dizziness, but my head spins from the sudden rush. Cameron's shoes shine in the light. The absurdity hits me: he polishes them in this ruined world and somehow has shoe polish.

"You look funny," I slur.

"Delene." He crouches, his face showing concern, and I fleetingly think he might be handsome if he weren't so freaking crazy. "You're fading. They extracted a lot of your blood."

"Well, wasn't that the idea? Bleed me dry to save others?" The metallic taste in my mouth grows stronger. "What did you change your mind about?"

"I'll release you for a few minutes. Drink something, stabilize."

Dizzy, I respond, "Why? You'll kill me anyway."

"You'll fare better standing. You can't last like this. Believe me."

Porter, to my right, speaks. "He's right. I've blacked out so many times I lost count."

I eye Cameron warily. "What do you want in return?" He always has an angle.

"I want..." He licks his lips and moves closer to me, way too close. "I want you to kiss me, and I want you to mean it."

Dizzy, I lift my eyebrows and shake my head. "Are you serious?"

He nods. "You've got ten minutes. That's five to get your blood regulated and drink water."

"Delene, do it," Porter shouts.

"Oh-okay," I manage.

Cameron moves, keying in commands at the computer behind me. A mechanical whir grates above and lowers me. Cameron supports my neck and back as the hook releases me. I'm a limp noodle.

My ankle cuffs remain, and while my hands are free, a pins-and-needles numbness tingles through my fingers.

Cameron is a good foot taller than me, at six-foot-four. He raises a meticulously plucked eyebrow.

"Well?"

I gulp. The bitterness in my mouth is at least up to the task at hand because otherwise, there is no way I could even touch him. I force myself to stand on tiptoe, pressing my mouth to his. Horrific images inundate my mind. He's deeply disturbed yet skilled at hiding it.

I fight the sickening mental pictures, sympathizing with his rough childhood yet repulsed by his cruelty.

Where River's kisses are passionate, Cameron's are lifeless and sloppy. I struggle not to pull away, aware Cameron idolizes Dr. Lytle. He seems to revel while I desperately want it to end. Cameron stands uncomfortably close, his breath heating my skin.

He is, however, wearing a toolbelt that holds his electrified baton.

Ignoring his memories, I bring my hands to his hips. His mind is a disjointed, scary space, but I pull him close and distract him with my lips.

When he moves closer, I respond convincingly because I know I must keep up the act for the sake of survival. I'd sooner kiss a rabid squirrel, but I act like he's setting me on fire, trailing my finger along his uniform shirt, down to his duty belt, and up his side. I zig-zag back toward his baton to distract him, which appears to work. He moans into my mouth, which makes me want to gag.

I keep going and cup his jaw with my free hand as I close my fingers around the top of his baton. His tentacle arms are busy with my backside, which is fine because he never sees what's coming.

Clear-headed, I yank his baton free. I press the button at the base and zap him in the stomach. Cameron sails back three feet, crashing to the ground.

"Good," Porter roars, "keep on him."

"Oh, don't worry. I will." I clutch the baton, advancing on Cameron as he groans and tries to get up. "That's for never helping me." I zap him again. "And that's for Lily." He convulses, then faints.

"Way to go, Delene," Porter cheers. "Hurry, get me down from here."

I drop the baton with a clatter and rush to the control panel.

A dizzying array of buttons and switches blur before my eyes, the machine as incomprehensible as if written in Russian. My fingers hover uncertainly over the controls. One wrong move could endanger Porter's life if I press the buttons in the incorrect sequence.

The shouts and pounding footsteps outside the door grow louder, our window for escape rapidly shrinking.

"I don't know which one will work," I shout, panicking. Precious seconds tick by as I struggle to decipher the controls that could free him. Porter meets my eyes with calm trust despite the fear darkening his pale face. His steadiness centers me. With a deep breath, I press the button on the left, praying it's the right choice.

The device above his mechanical restraints whirs to life. "Thank God," he huffs. "I was going to say the one on the left."

"A little late for that now."

"My bad."

The crane lowers him, and I cradle his neck as he lies on the ground.

I unholster his ankle cuffs, which take a minute because of their tightness. He plucks out the syringes in his arms with a grunt. "Cool. My turn." He helps me take mine off as well.

"Find a weapon. I'll guard the door."

"You got it." River's brother is his mirror image.

Porter pauses, blinking.

"Are you okay?" I ask. He rubs his forehead, then nods.

"Yeah. Help me stand, would you?"

"Sure." I help him to his feet, and he's the same height as his brother. I glance over my shoulder at Cameron's desk. "I think there's a drink on the desk if you want some. Might help."

"Thanks."

I scoot the baton off the floor and stand near the doors. Porter grabs Cameron's discarded soda can and chugs the rest, closing his eyes as the bubbly liquid soothes his parched throat. He's been suspended upside down much longer than I have, and it has depleted his body.

"Find a weapon of some kind. The gun, a knife, anything hard or useful."

"I'm on it." He checks the drawers, then disappears around the corner to the medical equipment area.

The door pounds behind my back like someone rammed it with a log. I jump and turn around with wide eyes as the door opens.

"*Delene.*"

River. He's panting like he's run a marathon. He cups my neck and presses his forehead against mine. I close my hands over him. "You found me. You came for me."

"Of course I did." He hovers his lips over my ear and confides, "I love you." I whisper the words back. I kiss him, a quick, feathery kiss.

"Don't I get a kiss, too?" We part, and I smile at Porter, who raises an axe. "I found this."

"*Porter?*" River staggers for breath and appears to cycle through myriad emotions—shock, relief, utter disbelief. "P—please tell me I'm not hallucinating."

"Well, unless you decided to eat those mushrooms in the forest Pops warned us about, nope." Porter grins.

River charges forward and locks Porter in a crushing bear hug. He whirls him around, tearful. "I can't believe you're alive. I thought I'd lost you." His voice breaks.

Porter returns the embrace, though far weaker. "Can't get rid of me that easily, Riv."

They cling to each other, reunited against all odds. I cup my mouth to hide my ear-splitting grin. River searches Porter's gaunt complexion as if re-memorizing every detail. "What happened? How are you here?"

Porter sighs, some of the light leaving his eyes. "It's a long story. I'll fill you in once we're safe." He winces, swaying.

The moment grounds River's shock. His brother is here but badly hurt. Questions will have to wait. Right now, Porter needs care. A clatter from the hallway rips me from the scene, and I stare out the doorway. "Guys, we've got company."

Chapter Twenty-Seven

River

"Close the door."

Technically, the hallway is our exit, and it's the only route I know because it's the one I came through.

Delene shuts the door, and I let go of Porter to help push a desk over as a barricade. I run a hand through my hair and spin around, searching wildly for another exit. The door I came through pounds. "There has to be another way out of here," Delene says.

I motion to the two doors which bracket either side of the room. "Try the one on the left. I'll get the one on the right."

"Okay." We hurry to both doors. "Mine's a supply closet," she calls back.

I inhale and open mine. A long hallway, not connected to the one I came through, spans straight ahead. "Lucky door number two. Come on." I support Porter, and Delene runs through the door.

She lowers her voice. "There's got to be an exit sign somewhere here."

We hurry through the hallway, and while my eyes rake the halls for any sign of an exit or door, we come to a fork at the end, standing left and right, with double doors to a stairwell ahead of us.

Porter curses. "Well, we're SOL. What do we do, bro?"

I meet Delene's eyes. "River, not the stairwell. That's the first place to look."

"They could come through either one." I deliberate between the two hallways. I peek through the slim window into the stairwell. Pops pushed Porter and me hard with workouts a few years ago and gave us whey protein. I still remember his praise about how strong we became.

I pass Porter to Delene and prepare to fly. "Take him and stay behind me. I have an idea."

"Better be a good one," Porter mutters.

I glare. "Is it ever not? Never mind, don't answer."

"Whoa, take it easy, bro. Wasn't about to say anything."

Footsteps echo in the stairwell below us, and Delene shifts her shoulders under Porter's arm to distribute his weight better.

"Are you sure about this?"

"Not a hundred percent, but we don't have many options."

A door slams from somewhere downstairs, overlapping the heavy footsteps and slap of magazines into rifles. "*Stop.*" Dr. Lytle's voice. "Tranquilize only. Live rounds are not permitted. I need them alive. Well, at least two of them. The injured one is disposable."

Porter gasps behind me. "Oh, thank you so much, Doc. Hey, Riv, remind me to send him a Christmas card once we get out of here."

"Yeah, I'll ship him a care package and a bag of coal."

"Do you remember that one day when Pops caught us stealing his knife to whittle slingshots? He was so pissed."

"Yep. This guy is different, though. Pops wasn't nuts."

"River," Delene says, "they're coming this way, too."

I check over my shoulder. Soldiers run toward us through the window further down the hall. Their frenzied yelling echoes louder, a hornet's nest poked with a stick. The soldiers below scale the stairs with slow movements, weapons trained on us.

"Give up," the soldier at the front yells, "you got nowhere to go."

I beat the air. "See, that's where you're wrong." I clench my fists and dive toward him. Before he pulls the trigger, I yank him by the collar, kick his weapon away, and fly to the top of the stairwell. I let him go, and he plummets to the ground, knocking over half his men. "Can you fly?" I ask Delene.

She unfurls with a sigh. "I think so." I get behind my brother and hook my arms under his, locking my hands around his chest.

"Okay. Follow me."

I dart past the scrambling men. Despite losing blood, Porter kicks a few soldiers as we fly by. I whoop as one goes down. Pops would be proud.

We pass Dr. Lytle with such speed he barely has a few seconds to move to the corner to avoid us.

"Head for the lobby floor," says Delene. I nod, my efforts focused on not dropping my brother. The momentum against the still stairwell air makes balancing his weight midflight easier.

We reach the lobby, Dr. Lytle and his men in pursuit, and bang open the doors. The main entrance is large enough to allow delivery trucks in.

"*Go,*" Delene urges. I hoist my brother, taking most of his weight over my shoulder, and run.

"Seal the door," Dr. Lytle barks behind us. A mechanical whir beeps, and the door closes as I haul Porter through.

Chapter Twenty-Eight

Delene

The steel doors grind as they slide closed with an electric hum. The gleaming metal is at least six inches thick—designed to contain dangerous specimens like me. I'll never make it through. So, I stop short, my heart pounding, and make a split-second decision.

"Go! I'll seal the door and be right behind you," I shout.

River hefts Porter's weight around his shoulder and hurries through the door. "Come on, Delene. We've *got* to go."

"I'll be right there," I repeat, and as the lie spills from my lips, I realize I'm trapped. But this can't be all for nothing.

Dr. Lytle, Cameron, and a handful of armed soldiers rush toward me, and my hand grazes the red button to seal the doors. I should be able to slip through in time. I'm going to try, anyway. I move to slam the button.

"Lily's *alive!*"

Whatever I expected Dr. Lytle might say to keep me here, this was not it. I stop dead in my tracks and stare. His intense eyes are wide and serious.

The two words coil around my heart, tiny tendrils of possibility taking root despite how much I shouldn't listen to him. "Y—you're lying."

"Am I?"

"Yes, you'll say anything to get me to stay. You're desperate."

"He's not lying," huffs Cameron. "I checked on her with two eyes this morning. She *is* alive."

This could be a trap. I keep my hand above the button as the soldiers await orders.

"Give up! Nowhere to go," one yells.

"Prove she's alive, and I'll give you whatever you want," I counter.

"I will. And you'll see Lily. Close the door first," says Dr. Lytle.

My thumb slams the bright red button before I can second-guess.

With a groan of protest, the steel doors slide closed, sealing my fate. River's panicked shouts echo from the other side, pleading with me to stop. Each cry is a dagger to my heart. I choke back a sob, forcing myself to block out his voice. I can't hesitate.

River has to live, even if it means I don't.

I harden my resolve. Whatever happens, I'll face it on my terms. But I can't rob River of his chance to escape while I still draw breath. I blink back tears as his cries fade. This is worth any sacrifice if River survives. This is my last stand.

I lift my chin defiantly as Dr. Lytle approaches. If this is my end, I'm taking him with me. River will live. I accept this fate without regret, my soul sustained by the simple power of love. I would do anything for River—even this.

"Go," I shout, voice breaking. "Meet at the cave."

It's another lie, but one that will save his life. Even as the doors lock, I have no regrets. I love him.

Chapter Twenty-Nine

River

I beat the impenetrable steel door, screaming for Delene. What is she thinking? There's no way out, though she claims she'll meet me at the cave.

"Riv." Porter yanks on my elbow while barely standing. "*River*, we gotta go, man. I need you. C'mon."

I scour the door, looking for a button or an entry panel. There must be a way back in.

"No." I peer into his eyes, conveying Delene's significance. Porter scans me. "Not without *her*."

"They're coming, man. She said she'd meet us, so she'll meet us. She can take care of herself, and she's tough. If we don't leave, we'll die."

I smack the door. "*Damn it!*" I hoist Porter's arm around my shoulder and race to the service van. We run past crumbling buildings and the charred pharmacy, looted during the medicine shortages.

The van's undetected, parked, and covered by a tarp in an alley, and the keys are in the ignition.

The thunder of heavy footsteps echoes on the pavement around the building. My eyes dart to the sky. If Porter could fly, he might have a fair chance. I could maybe carry him, but my muscles are on fire from the stairwell, and he weighs the same as me. We wouldn't get far, and they'd shoot us down. I scrub my jaw with my hand. I pull the door to the service van.

"Get in." I shove my brother through the door.

He sits in the passenger seat, ashen-faced and wiped. "I'm sorry I suck. I'm not going to be of much use."

I strap my seatbelt across my shoulders, tuck my wings in, and start the van. "You were plenty useful in helping me with those guards. Let me do the worrying. We'll rescue Delene." I shift the gear to drive, wiping my palms before letting off the brake. I dig my thumbs into the steering wheel padding. I trust Delene knows what she's doing. She escaped, and if there's one thing I know about her, she's a fighter. Guilt weighs on me. I came for Delene, but I left with my brother.

Porter puts on his seatbelt, rests his neck against the headrest, and looks at me. "You can get her if she doesn't come to us by nightfall. But bro, we gotta move."

I step on the gas and force Porter's head down as I charge the gate. The gate is not the same impenetrable steel. I'm going to ram through. I glance at Porter.

"Stay down no matter what."

"I will."

A line of soldiers zero their weapons at us. I hold the steering wheel steady, floor my foot, and duck. Three rounds hit the van, smashing the glass and whizzing over my head through the seat. Loud yells surround us as they jump out of the way.

We crash through the gate. My head rocks back with the impact.

A loud beeping noise blares. I'm covered with shards of glass, confused. How did I get this way? I slide my hand off the horn, and a nearby yelling grows louder. Porter grabs my shoulder, screaming to go. Shaking my head, I try to focus. I reverse and unstick the van from the gate, turn left, and floor it.

Pops didn't have enough time to teach us how to drive, not more than a simple lesson. His priority was teaching us to fight, comb forests and mountains for edible food, and hunt. I pull into traffic and realize I have no idea what I'm doing.

I drive worse than a blind man. Beside me, Porter looks terrified, even if he's cool enough to pretend he isn't. I did get behind the wheel once or twice, but I haven't had a lot of practice. I have no clue where to go. Hiding here won't last.

The mountains are to the east, straight ahead, so I make a few right turns, nearly crashing into traffic, but I get us as far away as we can. Porter slumps against the seat, holding on to the dash as I race through alleyways and busy streets.

The main gate in the fifty-foot-high concrete wall around the city is a few blocks away. Armed soldiers guard the impossible-to-breach border—they designed the wall to keep Evol-humans trapped inside. The only way out is to fly. I turn left sharply, stopping in a small alley where the van barely fits.

"How are you doing, man?" I ask. Porter needs medical attention. His eyes droop with a druggy kind of lethargy.

"Good to go," he slurs.

I'm weak from fighting and the crash but I move to get Porter. There's barely any room in the alleyway, and they'll be on us in minutes. Porter sighs, defeated, as I sling his arm around my shoulder and help him to walk.

"Leave me. You'll make it."

"No freaking way."

"There's no scenario where we're getting out of this, River. We're trapped."

I hobble down the alleyway with my brother and search for anywhere to go. "There's *always* a way out." I raise my left leg and kick a rusty door to my left. I'm sure someone saw us, but we keep moving. We enter a room scorched from floor to ceiling. Charred floorboards lie beneath us, spray paint covers the walls, and overturned furniture litters the space.

"Man, I've been thinking about a vacation. Great call. I'm giving this place five stars. Food's crap, though."

I give Porter a sharp glance. Now's not the time for jokes. "Shut up, dude, and let me think. Let me *think*." I survey the place, which appears to have been some shop a few decades ago. Is it a crackhouse dive or some drug depot? The musty and foul smell makes me want to gag, like something died, but there's no time to speculate. I hold on to my brother and clear the house from room to room. More tagged walls, burned floors, and a glass door leading to the streets, but nothing else. "Okay ... okay."

Porter grabs my shoulder. "What are we gonna do, Riv?"

I glance upward and see an additional structure above this one. Does it provide access to the roof? If we reach the top, we might be able to fly. A dull thump next door makes me cringe.

"Stay here," I whisper. Porter clutches an overturned couch to stay upright.

I linger by the corner of the doorway, my ears perked. Whoever is in there is dead silent. I lower my voice.

"Who's there?" I bark, menacing.

"Someone who can save your life." I expect Dr. Lytle's voice, not a kindly woman's.

I lift my eyebrows and peek around the corner. A woman in her sixties or seventies stands there, holding an M16-Nemesis X9. She has a long, white braid draped over her shoulder. She's wearing BDU fatigue pants, like Pops, and a black long-sleeved top. She's fit for her age. I notice an overturned, charred rug. Beneath it, a floor panel is ajar, revealing a secret space illuminated from below.

The faint seeds of hope take root, but I lower my eyebrows, not about to trust anyone. "Who are you?"

The woman smiles. She's got a disarming, somewhat optimistic attitude, considering our surroundings. "Why don't you two come with me and find out."

Chapter Thirty

Delene

My fists clench as Dr. Lytle stalks toward me, his shoes clicking ominously against the linoleum. Adrenaline spikes through my veins. Despite frantic shouts and gunfire outside, I stay focused. If there's even the slightest chance Lily still lives, I have to save her, no matter the cost.

Beside the doctor, Cameron flicks his baton on, his eyes lit with menacing eagerness. My stomach twists, thinking of all the times he pretended kindness while subjecting me to cruelty. While Dr. Lytle is deranged, his cruelty manifests openly, unlike Cameron, who hides his true nature behind a caring facade. This makes the doctor somehow less unsettling than Cameron's unpredictable malice.

I meet the doctor's stare and stand my ground. Lives hang in the balance, including my dear sister's. I don't dare back down now.

Dr. Lytle steps closer. I hover, weighing options. "Delene, you made the right decision. Let's talk. I'll let you visit your sister, but the question is, will you make this easy or hard?"

I draw in a long breath and fly to the floor.

Dr. Lytle stalks toward me, LEDs glinting off his silver hair. Kneeling, his condescending smile is replaced by a weary expression.

"Please cooperate, Delene." His pristine coat fails to mask the coppery blood scent. I sense his desperation. Is his life's work worth losing humanity?

He runs a frustrated hand through his hair when I don't respond. "Where are your friends going?"

"You don't need them. I'm in perfect condition," I insist.

Dr. Lytle stands and looks me over. "Resist, and we'll shoot. Cameron, take her to my office."

Cameron jabs me with his baton. "You're lucky I don't kill you," he hisses.

"Yeah, because then they'd kill *you*."

"Shut up." He pushes me harshly, grabs my elbow, and yanks me along the hall. "Come on."

Cameron escorts me down the sterile hallway to a slightly ajar door bearing Dr. Lytle's name.

I've never been to his office. I think of Lily, but I note the cluttered shelves lined with medical texts and anatomy models as we enter. An antique photo on the desk draws my gaze, so misplaced among the clinical trappings.

In the photo, a much younger Dr. Lytle beams next to a winsome brunette woman with two young children, a boy and a girl who look surprisingly similar to me, with blonde hair and mischievous expressions. They all smile brightly, bathed in dappled afternoon light outside somewhere—the picture of an idyllic family. *Kiddo. Angel.* For an instant, the syrupy moniker he gave me and his cheerful whistling tunes make sense, almost replacing the monster I've perceived with a man who once experienced happiness.

I barely digest this revelation before Dr. Lytle enters the room. Perhaps his family meant something to him once. But if any glimmers of humanity still linger, they are buried far too deep for me to reach or even contemplate. All I can do is endure his brutality and plan to escape someday.

Cameron chains me to the chair opposite Dr. Lytle's desk. Okay, he's not the brightest light bulb in the drawer, and judging by his wince, I almost regret duping and stunning him. Almost.

Dr. Lytle catches me looking at the framed photo. His fingers tremble as they trace the edges of the framed photograph, and his once impassive eyes darken with a storm of emotions he'd buried for years. The room is silent, save for the almost imperceptible catch in his breath. Memories, regrets, and the weight of past choices converge in that fragile second. He remembers laughter, warmth, the feeling of his daughter's tiny hand in his, and the pride he felt watching his son take his first steps.

A wistful sigh escapes him, a sound so unlike the hardened man he's become. But as quickly as the vulnerability appears, it's gone, replaced once again by the cold, unyielding mask of Dr. Lytle.

With a swift motion, he places the frame facedown, but not before I glimpse the tear that dared to escape his eye. He is both a monster and a broken man, haunted by the ghost of a life lost.

The faded picture of his family taunts him, a relic of the man he once was. Interesting. The corners of Dr. Lytle's mouth lift in a snarl even as his hands quiver, decades of buried trauma rising to the surface. Was his cruelty born from a childhood marred by pain? Or did the military poison his psyche, sacrificing his humanity for war?

He shakes it off, templing his fingers together, and then his lips purse in a dirty smirk. I might have pried into his past, but he's got me where he wants me. I'm at his disposal.

I stare over his shoulder, where next to his framed degrees and awards of commendation, my sister's speckled wings are mounted on the wall behind him like a prized fish.

I have no words.

My eyes shift back to Dr. Lytle.

"Oh, *those*. It's complete hubris to keep trophies and degrees from another lifetime ago, back in my heyday as a hotshot scientist. But what can I say? I'm sentimental. Something wrong, little angel?"

I tense and lower my voice. "I'm going to kill you."

He glances behind him with a relaxed sort of air and appraises his prize. "Ah. Trivial sentimentality. I plan to hang your wings above hers if it gives you solace. Then you'll never be apart."

I grit my teeth and lurch. There's nowhere to go, of course, and my chains rattle. All I manage to do is create pressure and pain in my shoulders and waist and elicit laughter from Dr. Lytle and Cameron, who stands near the door.

"What did you *do* with her?"

I shake my head. His *trophy* says it all. "At least tell me," I plead.

Dr. Lytle drums his fingers on his mahogany desk. "How about I *show* you?"

My eyebrows lower. "What are you talking about?"

He sighs and slides his tablet across the desk, busying himself. "This."

He turns the tablet to me, and my whole body grows still. In the video, my sister is on a white hospital bed in a spotless room. Her hair is a pale imitation of the lustrous locks I'd admired all my life. She looks like a frail human.

"Is ... is Lily alive?"

"That depends on your definition of 'alive.'"

I'm at his mercy. I'd do anything to save Lily. They paralyzed her wings before removing them, leaving her catatonic. She became their blood supply.

I fight back tears, staring at Lily onscreen.

"Name your price." Tears slide down my face.

Cameron stares hard, but I'm locked in an unblinking war with Lytle.

"You're hardly in a position to negotiate." His kitten-soft, menacing patience locks back in place.

"I will fight every step of the way if you try to force me." I hate that I'm crying in front of him. But the tears won't stop. *Oh, Lily, what have they done to you?* I plead to take her place.

A wave of guilt crashes over me for leaving him, but he has his brother, and I have my sister. Sort of. My eyes shift to Lily on the screen, and I fight back tears. Her skin has taken on a gray hue reminiscent of morning clouds. There's hardly anything left. "You've used her as much as you can." I don't mask my disgust about their actions or her lovely, speckled wings mounted above his head like a trophy. "Take me instead."

Dr. Lytle looks me over, calculating.

"Please, let Lily go," I beg. "I will give you anything."

His eyes drop, scanning me. I'm healthier than when they kept me in the lab. My skin gives a healthy glow after fresh air, sunshine, and eating steadily. Thanks to River and the excellent care he took of me, I appear more robust.

Cameron steps forward. "Delene, no."

"Stay out of this," I hiss, turning back to Dr. Lytle. "What'll it be?"

He drags his nails across the desk.

"You're offering to be harvested. Are you certain?"

"I know what I'm doing. I'll give anything to save Lily," I reply firmly.

"Your sister is at death's door, Delene. She's in no condition."

I glare. "Then there's no deal. I will fight you."

"Let me think." Dr. Lytle rubs his chin, deliberating. "I'll give you two days with her. She's in no shape to leave."

"We heal fast," I bite back. "Without being tortured and having medicine to help Lily heal, her resilience might surprise you."

"Two days." He points at me. "During that time, I want one pint of blood a day from you to make up for what we won't be getting from her."

"Okay. But I want healthy meals for Lily and good medicine. If she's well enough to leave, I want her fully released and left alone for the rest of her life."

He expels breath through his nose. "You do realize what you're doing here, right? Because we won't go easy on you. I will take as much blood as you can give. You'll be a shell of a person."

I lean forward as far as the chains will allow. "My life for hers."

"Very well."

He leans over me to grab a tablet from the desk. I lift my hands as much as the restraints allow and clamp them over his wrist. His eyes widen in shock, but I do not lessen my hold. I search his eyes, and shuffled images and memories fill me. *His* memories.

My fingers graze against Dr. Lytle. I'm in a dimly lit room where a young boy, presumably Lytle, cowers in the corner, tearful eyes reflecting a world of neglect and cruelty. He whistles a familiar chipper tune, burying the ache of his childhood deep within.

The scene morphs, and I witness a young man, clad in military garb, screaming amidst chaos and gunshots, the scars of war etched into his psyche. Then, the most vivid of them all: his immersion, eyes wild and frantic, engrossed in the lure of scientific discovery and the intoxicating allure of unparalleled glory.

I see his wedding to his gentle wife, who suffers from low self-esteem, and the moment they learned their daughter had leukemia.

In the memories, Dr. Lytle cradles his daughter's frail form in a dimly lit room. Her once vibrant hair lies thin and sparse on the pillow, her cheeks sunken. Yet those brilliant blue eyes look up at him, still filled with trust. His wife, a woman who battled with her worth, sits on the edge of the bed. With eyes swollen from endless tears, she absentmindedly twists the ring he gave her on their wedding day.

Once unspoken and masked by insecurities, their love now binds them in this shared pain.

"Why can't you just let it out?" she sobs, voice choked with emotion. "Why can't you cry with me?"

Dr. Lytle's jaw tenses, holding back the storm within. He's been the fortress throughout this heart-wrenching ordeal, never wavering, never revealing his devastation. I feel her longing for him to break, to share this anguish. But then, I see him, later, alone in the house's silence, retreating to his study where he lets his sorrow consume him, mourning for his lost daughter. The depth of his grief resonates, raw and profound.

I move deeper and clutch onto one memory from long ago. In a sterile, white room, two soldiers sit in metal chairs side-by-side. "FAIRBORNE" and "SHAW" are stitched on their army uniform pockets. Their rank badges are missing from their lapels, likely removed intentionally. Dr. Lytle makes notes on the clipboard as he sits. I recognize my grandfather, who is hardly five years older than me. His hawk-like gaze and closely cropped, military-cut blond hair pale beneath the light.

Next to him, the handsome, dark-skinned man chuckles and examines his nails. "You know, it's crazy. I haven't had chapped skin or dry lips since we came to the program. Usually, in winter, I use a lot of lotion, but it's weird, like I don't need anything."

Dr. Lytle speaks from where he sits. "I expect you won't have to ever again. And as soon as we finish treatment, you will function well at high altitudes, no matter where you find yourselves."

My grandfather shifts in his seat with a slight shake of his head. "This is amazing. It's like I'm a superhero."

"You are," Dr. Lytle says. "And by the time we finish, you'll be able to do things you never even *dreamed* of."

Lytle's past echoes: The military superiors who sent him to war told him sacrifice was the only way to save humanity. Their doctrine still drives him today, blinding him to morality.

I release his wrist, pulling away. I catch my breath as his memories detach. His past staggers me. My disdain shifts to uneasy pity.

The revelation doesn't absolve him of his heinous actions by any means. Still, it paints him in a different light—one of a broken man driven to extremes by the traumas he endured. My resolve wavers, caught between the line of empathy and anger. How does one reconcile the monster within?

I narrow my eyes. "You peddled lies."

He's pale and frozen. I shake my head.

"Tell me something, Dr. Lytle. Did you know we would be born with wings?"

He straightens his coat and rubs his wrist, eerily calm. "Oh, I knew everything. I had the evolution mapped out. And if we hadn't gone to war and destroyed everything, I would be the richest and most successful scientist alive. And *you* would have been born on Mars or Io. But here we are."

I stare, furious. "Here we are." He pushes back and stands.

"Can I get you a magazine?"

I'd love to rip him to shreds.

"No? Okay. Back in two ticks. Stay right there." He cheerfully opens a side door and disappears through.

Speechless, I stare hard at Lily's wings. The hair on my neck rises, and I become aware of Cameron ogling me by the corner window.

I've got much bigger problems, like survival as a human vegetable. Still, I stretch my lips, trying to look appealing. Cameron's got a thing for me, and staying on his good side might be in my best interest. He waggles his eyebrows, then pushes off from the corner and approaches me. He leans in close as if he's about to kiss me again. I try not to recoil. His breath heats my skin, inches from my mouth.

But he surprises me and parks his mouth near my jaw.

His lips tickle the shell of my ear, paralyzing me. "Delene," he whispers, "I have the night shift. No matter what Dr. Lytle does, I'll make you pay for fighting back. Karma always comes around. From tonight on, you're mine."

He kisses my cheek.

I won't give him the satisfaction of a response. I always knew something in him was missing. Without the war, they'd lock Cameron up, not me. Dr. Lytle may be psychotic, but at least he's openly insane.

Chapter Thirty-One

River

"Come on," the woman urges. "We've no time to waste."

Porter appears beside me, an eyebrow raised in silent inquiry. With a sigh, I guide him to the trapdoor. "Seems we don't have a choice."

"I'm Glenda Navarro-Walking Bear," the old woman introduces herself.

"River and Porter Sh—"

"Shaw," she interjects. "I know."

As Porter moves to descend, I grip his elbow. "How do you know our names?" Glenda knows a lot about us.

A playful grin curves her lips, casting a radiant glow on her face. The subtle lines that trace her expression hint at a beauty that once turned heads in her youth. She slings her rifle over her back and puts a hand on her hip. "You both remind me so much of your grandpa."

"You knew Pops?" Porter's voice carries a hint of surprise.

Glenda's expression turns nostalgic. "I served with him. We were part of the original trial team." Memories of Pops flood in. Anyone speaking fondly of him is someone he must've trusted. "Now, get moving."

Porter begins his descent. The stairway, worn from countless footfalls, shows signs of age. Dusty cables and rusted pipes line the stone walls, remnants of a forgotten underground system.

She pulls a chain, shutting the trap door above us, sealing us in. Objects fumble close to where she stands, and a distinct scratch echoes in the dark as she strikes a match. Glenda cups the match flame, shielding it from the cold. She brings the flame to the wick of a lantern perched on the top step.

"Come on, then."

I catch Porter's eye in the dimness. He trusts her, and that's good enough for me. Porter's always read people well.

Our swaying lantern scatters sinister shadows. "The city abandoned this subway due to budget cuts before the war. They started it from beneath the downtown temple, but it never expanded once the war started. It later became our hidden trading spot. Stick close."

As we traverse, I notice bags piled against walls and the occasional lanterns marking our path. "I need to find a safe place for my brother. And I need to go back for—"

She interrupts, "The girl?"

Porter chuckles. "She's sharp, River."

"What do you know about us?" I probe further.

Glenda's response carries a playful undertone. "You're unmistakably Shaw's descendants, River. We've kept a watchful eye, waiting. I'm well aware of Porter and Delene. She escaped before we could rescue her last week, but your showing up was a fortunate twist."

Reassured, I nod.

"A few minutes more," Glenda calls back. "Then food and water, and we can go over the plan."

"What plan? Will you help us save Delene?"

"Oh no." Glenda brings the lantern to shoulder level, the amber light distorting her kind features into something more sinister.

"Whoever said anything about rescuing anyone? We're going to blow the lab to kingdom come."

"Whoa, whoa. Time *out*." Porter stops walking.

Pausing, I rub my stiff neck, feeling the day's weight. Glenda shoots me an impatient glance. "We can't dawdle, River. Your presence was no small diversion."

Frustration seeping in, I counter, "If you went to such lengths for us, why not for Delene?"

"Because clearly, she can handle *herself*," Glenda says in a matter-of-fact tone. "We have bigger problems. Come on."

I stay rooted. "Delene *is* my problem. And I'm not leaving without her."

Glenda grits her teeth. "*Ay, Dios mio.* Listen, there may be a way to get you in and extract her before we detonate the bombs. Hurry, we don't have much time." She turns and strides ahead, not waiting to see if we follow. "Keep close unless you inherited night vision."

Porter shrugs. "Your call."

Glancing at Glenda's retreating figure, I know we must follow. Her lantern casts shifting shadows across the tunnel walls—our best option, though not ideal. Dr. Lytle better not hurt Delene. I drape my brother's arm around my shoulder and hurry to catch up.

We trail Glenda another five minutes through the decaying tunnel before turning left, where the track branches off. Ahead, the abandoned rails stretch into darkness. Rivulets of water trickle down the concrete walls, pooling on the litter-strewn floor. The loamy, moldy scent lingers. Porter sweats beside me. "He needs water. Can we stop?"

She regards me over her shoulder. "It's a few minutes away. Keep going."

I pat Porter's hand. "Come on, P. A little bit further."

"You always were good at having my back," wheezes Porter.

A milky-blue light shines far ahead. "Where are you taking us?" I ask.

I search around to ensure no one follows. Glenda turns off the lantern. "Not far now," she says, shouldering Porter's weight.

I look over, uncertain. "Are you sure you can handle my brother? He's big."

A large amount of the weight lifts from my shoulders, lightening the load. Glenda pulls Porter's arm around her. "Of course. I'm an Evol-human, like you. First-generation, still strong as an ox. Let's hurry and get him some medical attention and food."

I side-eye my brother. "Are you doing okay, P?"

Panting, he waves me off with a hand on my shoulder. Together, we approach the light at the tunnel's end and discover a large train station with a semicircle of once-thriving shops transformed into makeshift homes.

I don't know what I expected, but a large group of thirty to fifty winged Evol-humans of all ages and colors is not it.

My mouth goes dry as I take in the bustling underground platform. Dozens of figures with striking wings flutter about their business. I scan the luminous glowstones lighting up shopfront lean-tos packed into the abandoned tunnels. Children's echoes, vibrant melodies, ripple through the curved walls. After a lifetime alone, this community of winged beings staggers me.

Before the war, rumors spread of a utopian city where the wisest scientists had constructed an undersea habitat safe from the ravages of war and plague. I've wondered if the underwater Evol-humans took over. We've heard tales of nomadic clans roaming the wastelands, staking claims on abandoned cities, but no one knows if they survived.

The distant settlements might still harbor other Evol-humans, but the vast emptiness makes it hard to believe. Stumbling upon a real community is like stepping into a dream.

Two eager Evol-human children flutter across the tracks, warming my heart. I wave, amazed. I have never seen children like us. I take in the details of this underground settlement, mind blown.

"This is my favorite part. Welcome home," Glenda beams on the other side of my brother. Porter is weak, but his awe and amazement at our reception transform into joy.

A handsome Latino man in his thirties flies down the tracks, accompanied by two other Evol-humans. His wings are striking—sleek black feathers tipped with intricate white patterns.

"Porter," Glenda says, "this is my son Alejandro. He's a doctor who treated many of our ailing people in the tunnels. I want you to go with him—he'll take excellent care of you." Alejandro gives Porter a reassuring nod, his keen eyes already assessing how to best nurse my brother back to health. Though only a few years older than us, Alejandro seems like a gifted healer.

Porter and I exchange glances. I tell him to go. He needs medical attention, and I'm anxious to return to Delene. The two men with Alejandro support Porter on either side and fly off with him.

"Don't worry," Alejandro says. "We will take good care of your brother."

"Make sure he gets something to eat."

Alejandro nods and flies off in the same direction. Glenda ascends a stepladder to the platform leading to the houses.

"This way. There's not a lot of time." I fly to the tracks. Winged Evol-humans dart and fly over. They hurry, packing blankets and clothes into bags and shutting cases as we pass.

"Where are they going?" I ask.

"Don't worry about that," Glenda says sharply. "Come on."

I gulp, not accustomed to so many people. They *are* my people. I get back to business and focus on Delene. Where is she? Is she okay?

"How many of you are here?"

"You and your brother make forty-seven."

I raise my chin and stare. "And Delene?"

"If we get her out in time, forty-eight."

She ushers me into a cluttered room filled with weapons and tactical gear. A model of the city rests on a central table. I run a hand through my hair and study Glenda. This gung-ho crap is everything I've stayed away from. What would Pops make of this?

"How is blowing everything up supposed to help us? Cut off the serpent's head, and two more grow." The Book of Pops has never steered me wrong. Glenda understands the reference.

She meets me head-on, resolute. "Taking out their main source and equipment will cripple them."

I consider this. I want Delene back, but at what cost? Despite the awe of finding others like us, this underground world feels stifling. I stare at the miniature replica, roiling inside. Something about this doesn't sit right with me. I don't want to get into this war. Finding so many others like us is extraordinary, but living underground with no fresh air and dingy tunnels to fly through? The thought depresses me. I want to be far away from here, in panoramic skies and fresh air. And as ridiculous as Delene's idea of an island sounded, it's getting more appealing.

I grip the table's edge, lean forward, and look at Glenda. "Tell me how we get in."

Glenda runs a finger along the table's model paths, illustrating as she speaks. "We have an inside man who delivers food, and he's worked as a server in the kitchen for years. He was born without wings, so nobody's ever suspected him."

A slender young man with clean-cut brown hair enters, carrying a tarnished silver tray. A cracked ceramic bowl contains a thin vegetable soup, the wooden spoon sticking straight up like a mini mast, flanking a chipped glass of cloudy water, and a crusty heel of bread on faded cloth napkins. He sets the tray in front of me and holds out his hand.

I return the handshake. "River, this is Adam. He's going to take you there, and he'll show you where they're keeping Delene."

"Hi," Adam says. "I brewed the formula for the IV fluid for the Evol-humans in the lab. I've never been there, but I know what room they keep her in."

Chapter Thirty-One

I nod. "Thank you. When is this going to happen?"

"Tonight," Glenda says.

"And say this works. What's the plan after we get Delene and you blow everything up? Won't they come looking for you?"

"They'll have their hands full with the repercussions of the blast. And while they do, we'll go through the tunnels to the mountains. There's a sewage drain door at the mouth of the canyon, and we're heading there as soon as I receive confirmation." She motions to the soup in front of me. "Eat. You'll need your strength."

I lift the spoon to my mouth and eat the soup, which is chicken noodle flavored. I've eaten fresh game for so long that the processed flavor tastes strange, though I like the salt in the broth.

"Everything is ready to go," Glenda continues. "You'll both leave in an hour. River, Adam will get you in and show you where to go." She grows serious, her eyes tearful. I pause, the spoon halfway to my mouth. "You'll have twenty minutes," she says. "We chose a time with the fewest casualties. Our target is primarily Dr. Lytle and his men. Fewer people are on the night shift, and those who work tend to deal directly with the harvesting."

"I understand. Tell me where to go, and I'll get Delene."

We assess each other in silent agreement. Pops once told me if you're ever in stressful situations, always look for the quieter, unruffled people. I'm worried, but I take comfort in Adam's observant mien. He couldn't have passed for a staff member without being good at self-preservation, and he acts wily and agile. I need him to help me rescue Delene.

The soup tastes old and the bread stale, but I wolf the food down. From a sideways glance, Alejandro examines Porter as he sits on a stool, shining a light into his eyes. He'll be okay if I leave him here until I rescue her. I'll get her out.

Chapter Thirty-Two

Delene

"Let me see her."

Dr. Lytle scratches his jaw with his thumb. "All right, but there's no guarantee she'll be awake. She's far gone, and she comes and goes."

I resist the impulse to attack him. How is he so calm? I swallow my anger and follow him down the hall, Cameron prodding my back. There's that to deal with, too. His resentment channels into me. Cameron's never lost it, but a cold, silent white rage thickens the air, and my hackles rise. Did I underestimate him?

As Dr. Lytle escorts me down the sterile hallway, I chance a sideways glance at him. His polished shoes click rhythmically, his strides unhurried. What inner demons drive this man? My thoughts drift to the faded photo I glimpsed in his office—Lytle as a happy father cradling his children. Perhaps that man still exists somewhere beneath the monster.

"Did you have a family once, Dr. Lytle?" I ask softly.

He flinches, a brief flash of vulnerability crossing his face like a slipping mask. But it's gone in an instant, extinguished. "Long ago," he says tersely. "You remind me of my daughter, but the past doesn't matter now."

His clipped tone reveals everything. This crusade consumes him, but at what cost? Even the most hardened hearts yearn for connection. Perhaps appealing to that lonely, lost father is the only way to reach him.

We enter room 216 through a sealed door, seventh on the right, and the breath leaves my body at the sight of my sister.

Lily rests in a hospital bed to the left, her pallor contrasting starkly with the fiery strands of her unkempt red hair sprawled across the pillow. Despite the pervasive smell of bleach, the unmistakable odor suggests she hasn't cleaned in far too long.

Tears fill my eyes, and I shuffle to Lily's bedside in my restraints. "Lily? Lily, it's me. It's Delene." She's asleep, but her eyebrows raise. She heard me. I lean down and press a soft kiss on her forehead. "You're coming with me." I then zero in on Dr. Lytle. "Let her go."

"We will, as soon as she regains consciousness. In case you haven't noticed, she's not up to par."

"Thanks to you," I snarl.

Unfazed, he tilts his head. "Semantics, Delene. It's about survival. Harvesting Evol-human blood is the only way to save humanity. You may think of me as a monster, but many consider me a hero."

"Hero? Even *parasites* don't call themselves saviors when they feed off their hosts. But then again, you're in a whole different category."

He smirks, amused. "Always sharp, right? Sit by your sister."

I scan the vacant bed beside Lily, overshadowed by the intimidating array of medical gear. How many had lain there before? What happened to them? River had been unsure about Porter's fate, and I'd feared the worst for my sister. Looking at Lily, frail and fading, my heart aches. But she's breathing, and a spark ignites in me. There's a chance. I stare at her as I sit. Once Cameron uncuffs me, I graze my finger along Lily's upper arm.

Her memories wash over me—rage and anguish.

They paralyzed her wings with an epidural before removing them, leaving her catatonic. She became a blood bag they could tap at their leisure.

Cameron yanks me back to my bed. I glare with all the hatred I can muster. I'll never forgive them for what they've done. He swabs my arm, focused intently on his work. His hands tremble as he sanitizes the injection site. Our eyes meet, and I sense the conflict within him. He's an outcast who found purpose working for Dr. Lytle. But at what cost to his soul? Still, perhaps some scrap of goodness remains.

"You're hooking me up to drain my blood already?" I ask incredulously.

"Well, we did take your sister off the transfusion as agreed," Dr. Lytle replies with an indifferent shrug. "You said it yourself, your life in exchange for hers. We need a new donor now. Congratulations, you've been selected as lucky contestant number two."

He gives me a smile that makes my skin crawl. "So, let's get those tubes in you, kiddo."

I shake my head. *You unbelievable monster.* What kind of life did he have as a child? I glimpsed his dodgy military career and how he wormed through the ranks to become a decorated officer before he spearheaded the Evol-human initiative, but how did he grow up? He has such a kind, open face, the type of guy you *know* is trustworthy, with a pleasant, witty voice. My heart transforms into a lead ball in my chest. Beneath his monstrous deeds, Dr. Lytle is still a man.

And men have flaws.

"What?" he asks when I stare too long.

"Nothing. I'm trying to decide whether you're deranged or full-on insane."

He chuckles and checks my sister's pulse. "Have you come to any conclusions?"

"The jury's still out," I seethe. "Stop touching Lily."

He lifts his hand from her wrist. "Take it easy, Delene. I want to make sure she's still with us. Cameron, get me an epinephrine syringe. I'm going to wake her."

Cameron pauses as he's about to inject me with the blood transfusion IV. "Do you want me to get the Epi-pen before or after I stick her?"

"Before." Dr. Lytle meets my eyes. "A promise is a promise."

When Dr. Lytle turns, Cameron leans over Lily with a syringe. I take the opportunity and choke him from behind. His arms flail, and he fights me, but my father taught me to fight well. The tranquilizer from earlier has worn off, and I fly high, determined, using the force of gravity against his strength. He makes a rattling noise, and Dr. Lytle turns around, stunned.

"Don't do it," he warns. We struggle to the other side of the room, and I've cut off Cameron's air. He's a big guy, almost River's size, and holding his weight takes all I have. Dr. Lytle moves toward me but lingers by Lily as if he's changed his mind. Cameron's flesh turns blue, but I don't relent. If I don't stop, he'll die. I've never killed somebody, but if it's Lily and me against him and Dr. Lytle, I have no problem. He's a selfish, horrible human being who's done awful things.

"Delene?" Sweat pours over my forehead as I struggle with Cameron. I stare at Dr. Lytle. His hands clench Lily's slim throat. "Let him go," he warns softly. "I can snap her neck like *that*."

He's not lying. I've shuffled through his memories. Cameron gives a final rattle, and then his head lolls forward. I release him, and he drops to the floor in a lifeless heap. Extending my hands, I charge Dr. Lytle, punching him swiftly.

The momentum sends him flying backward, away from Lily. He grabs my arm with a fierce, viselike grip, the more experienced fighter with years of military training under his belt. Meanwhile, I'm restrained at the wrists and ankles, woefully unprepared. His face twists into a mask of deranged anger, hardened by cruelty. He closes his hand around my neck, and I beat my wings against him, fighting for my life.

Chapter Thirty-Three

River

The ride in the back of Adam's truck is bumpy and uncomfortable. Wedged between rice barrels, I shift my weight as he drives recklessly. The truck stops, but there's no noise through its thick walls. Half an hour later, the doors open.

"Hurry," Adam urges. "There's no time."

I leap from between the drums and exit the truck. We're in an underground parking lot.

"Kitchens are this way," he says. "Stay behind me by at least ten feet and hide if you hear someone."

I search around, ensuring no one follows. Adam walks with a purpose, pushing a food transport. He slams his palm on a button. Double doors reveal the Stockade. With a finger flick, Adam gestures for me to follow. I stay behind boxes, careful. Someone calls him. I duck behind stacks until their exchange ends and the greeter leaves.

"Come on, River." I follow Adam through the storeroom. He leads me to a supply closet and closes the door. A light sensor above us switches on, and shelves of cleaning supplies surround us. Adam gives me a key card and a gun. "She's in room 216 on the second floor. After your earlier spectacle, the guards have increased, so tear outta here at full throttle."

"I will."

"You're going to have to, man. You have less than 19 minutes to get in there, do whatever you're going to do, and get your girl. I'll be in the van, ready to go, and if you're not there in fifteen minutes..." He hesitates. "I'll leave without you."

"I understand. I'll be there."

"I hope so. Here." He places his ID card and lanyard in my hand and takes off his wristwatch, setting a fifteen-minute timer. He fixes the watch on my left wrist and hands me the lanyard. "This key card will get you back down here, and we'll leave the same way we came in. So, your mission is to get the girl and get in the van. When the timer hits zero, I get out of Dodge, with or without you. If we separate, go through the safe house to the tunnels. You'll have four minutes before the explosion detonates, so I suggest getting here pronto. Got it?"

I fit the lanyard around my neck and eye the timer. "Got it. See you soon." I extend my fist, and Adam knuckle-bumps me.

"Good luck."

"Luck isn't a strategy."

In the van, I'd already decided that, without hesitation, I'll shoot anyone who tries to stop me. I ignore the elevators, heading for the stairwell's cover instead.

I rush to the door, an X9 barrel in my face. I duck, moving swiftly as a blast goes off. I push the rifle away, clocking the guy's face and grabbing the gun as he's distracted. I strike him hard with the rifle's butt. He drops, unconscious, but pounding footsteps warn me of more. I pocket my handgun and grip the X9 tighter.

"Drop the weapon!" a shout comes from above.

"You're in my way," I retort. "Move, or I'll make you."

"Nowhere to run, kid. Hands up and back away nice and slow. Don't make me shoot."

"Just want the girl," I say. "Back off, or you're next."

His rifle points at me. "*Last* chance!"

I clip his shoulder, disarming him. Taking his weapon, I charge upstairs. Pops had a rule: point a gun only if you're ready to use it. Right now, I have every reason. I kick the door open. Five soldiers rush at me. I shift to semi-auto and fire, aiming to incapacitate. Thanks to Pops's training, they're down but breathing.

Screw this war. "Stop shooting. Get out or pay the price." I dodge bodies, sprinting to room 216. A young guard is inside, fear in his eyes. He's younger than me.

"Step aside," I command.

He's just a kid, scared and in over his head. Our uniforms may differ, but we're the same. We are tired of this war.

"Look," I say, lowering my weapon slightly, "I just want my girl. Move, and no one else gets hurt."

"She's all yours, man. God bless." He sags in relief and scurries past without a word. He flees, and doubt crosses my mind. How can we ever find peace if we don't find humanity among our enemies? I cast aside my thoughts and turn around. First, I need to get Delene to safety. Then, I'm going to need a whole lot of therapy.

"Yo."

The terrified soldier stops and looks at me.

The other soldiers on the floor behind him scrape themselves up. I speak loudly. "The building's going to explode. You've got ten minutes. Save who you're going to save."

The guard, ashen, helps another soldier flee. Two of them stare, still on the ground, but I shake my head and pat my rifle. "Don't. I'm not here for you. You'll die if you stay. Get out." One gets to his feet with a wince and limps down the hall. None of them are in any position to fight back, and as soon as I'm confident they won't attack, I focus on the doors.

I swipe Adam's key card, and the doors open. Delene fights for her life, turning scarlet as Dr. Lytle chokes her. I fire a warning shot. He doesn't let go.

I advance, pointing the X9 at him. "*Let her go.* Take your hands off her throat."

He closes his fingers around her neck even more, and Delene gags. "No. I don't think I will. Lower the weapon, and we'll talk." Behind him, a redheaded girl stirs, looking his way.

"She can't breathe. Release her, or I'll shoot."

Delene wheezes, and he relaxes his tense grip though his hands stay around her throat. The redhead behind him takes a thick tube on the bed beside her and raises on her knees. "Lower the weapon, son," Dr. Lytle orders. I raise my free hand and bring the X9 down by my side. The redhead is zombie-like, with circles under her eyes. Lily. She winds the tube around her fists and lifts the cord over his head.

She's so ghostly, quiet, and pale I'm unsure if she's real. Maybe the crackhouse had some airborne drug that messed with my head. Dr. Lytle pulls Delene in front of him like a shield, his hands still around her neck, and gives me a cold, hard stare. "Put the weapon on the ground, kid, and step back, or I'll snap her neck." She shakes her head.

"River, don't."

"*River*?" Dr. Lytle brightens. "River. Your face looks mighty familiar. Unless you managed to get a haircut in the last few hours, I bet your last name is *Shaw*. Well, how do you like that? I'm getting the twofer special today, aren't I? I didn't roll out of my nice, warm bed this morning thinking about replacing my living vegetables with their siblings, but shucks, I'll take i—"

The tube around his neck effectively cuts his air, which the girl behind him yanks tight. He lets go of Delene and struggles. Lily's pin-thin limbs look as strong as limp noodles, but her face contorts, and she holds him firm.

Behind Lily, a long knife appears. "Let him go," a soldier barks, emerging behind her. "Do it now."

I lift my rifle and train it on the soldier, but I don't have a clear shot.

"No. Kill me," Lily gags.

I take a step forward. "I have a shot, man. Let her go and walk away."

The soldier presses his blade to Lily's throat, his crazed eyes shining. A tiny pearl of blood blooms at the knifepoint. "One move and she dies."

Delene calls my name, pulling me from the brink.

I drop my weapon. How can Delene and I recover if her sister dies? But she grabs the rifle before it hits the floor and shoots the soldier. Lily tightens her hold on Dr. Lytle, her resolve restored.

He passes out, and she lets him fall to the floor.

I meet Delene's frightened eyes and help her stand, compassion tempering my revenge. With deep breaths, I step away from Lytle's body. Delene's hand steadies as she aims.

"Turn Lily away," she says. "I'll finish this."

I hesitate for a split second, but Delene's resolved gaze leaves no room for debate. She needs to face this demon on her own. Without a word, I pivot and shield Lily, who crumbles to the floor in tears. I cover her ears just in time.

A gunshot rings out. When I look up, Dr. Lytle lies motionless while Delene stands over him, eyes haunted. She's ended a life but saved countless more. Silently, I reach out, offering her my hand without judgment. She grasps it.

Together, we step into our future.

Chapter Thirty-Four

Delene

The single gunshot splits the air—sharp, quick. Dr. Lytle crumples, lifeless. We stare at his body—the man who inflicted such torment gone in an instant.

My hands tremble, the heavy rifle an unbearable weight. I've taken a life. I glance at Cameron's stiff form. No, *two*. My stomach knots.

River touches my shoulder, solemn. "It had to be done. It's over."

In the distance, alarms blare to life. Shouts rise, footsteps pounding.

They're coming for us. River takes my hand.

I let the gun fall—regret and relief clashing within.

River checks the time. "Less than ten minutes." Stepping over Dr. Lytle, he retrieves the gun and touches my cheek. I block out the world, lost in his palm's warmth. "Are you okay?"

I nod and massage my throat. "I'm all right. Help me get Lily up." I stare at Lily, who looks near death despite her anger as she strangled Dr. Lytle. She blinks, and I notice her eyes have the same shade as mine, what our grandma called the heart of the ocean. You forget little details when someone you love is away. "Come on, sweetie," I soothe as I help her off the bed.

River takes her other arm. "You're Delene's sister?" Lily nods, on the verge of passing out.

I grip her tighter. "Hang on to us."

"Who is this?" she motions to River.

"Lily, this is my boyfr ... my, uh, River."

"*Boyfriend?*" River asks with a hopeful tone.

I push my hair out of my face, embarrassed. "I didn't say that."

"It sure sounded like you were *going* to. And I wouldn't have a single problem with that title." He lifts his eyebrows.

"Really?"

"Really." He nods to Lily. "Nice to meet you, but I gotta be honest, the circumstances suck." The corners of Lily's mouth lift, but she's ashen-faced. River frowns. "Where are her wings?"

"They removed them," Lily says weakly. "The monster mounted them ... in his office. Delene, I need an adrenaline shot, or I won't last."

"I've got it."

River holds Lily upright as I discover a syringe on the silver medical tray by the bed. I lean over Lily, syringe in hand. She meets my eyes and sucks in a breath, bracing herself.

"Ready?"

Lily gives a tight nod, her face pale but resolved. "Do it."

I press the needle into her outer thigh muscle. She flinches, squinting against the pain. River grips her shoulder, keeping her steady as I push the plunger in. She's complete skin and bones, and though she's older and taller, she weighs at least twenty pounds less.

"You okay?" I ask.

Lily lets go of me. "Yeah ..." Her pupils dilate, and she stands straighter.

"What did you give her?" River raises an eyebrow.

"It's an adrenaline shot Cameron gave me the few times I was too weak to continue as a prisoner. The adrenaline will get her out of here, and then we can treat her."

River peers into Lily's eyes. She's able to stand and walk, so he releases her. "Are you going to be okay on foot?"

"I think so."

"Let's go, then." River leads us to the doorway. "This place is going to blow sky high."

My eyes widen. "When?"

"In less than eight minutes. We've got to *move*. Follow me and stay close."

"Okay."

River raises the rifle as we run through the door down the hall. "Jeez, I guess my warning worked," he mutters as we approach the vacant stairwell. We take the stairs.

I stay by Lily just in case, but she's okay. We wait on the top step while River secures the area.

"All clear." He pauses to check his watch. "Crap."

"What is it?"

"The timer is stuck on ten minutes." He looks at us. "Hurry. I don't know how long it's been stopped. Lily, can you run?"

"I'll try," she puffs. Lily tucks an unruly strand of copper hair behind her ear, a familiar nervous habit since childhood. Her fingers work at a loose thread on her tunic. "Dee, can we trust these people?"

"Yeah, we can. Come on." We speed our stride, hand-in-hand and run for it.

"There's no telling how off the timer is," River pants, "Adam might have already left."

"Adam?"

River pushes the double doors to the parking lot, and a man by a van hollers, frantically waving us over. Distant shouts and the pound of footfalls increase as the soldiers close on us.

"Go," River huffs, pushing my back. Lily and I run past. I glance over. Lily grits her teeth, and sweat pours down her face. My heart races as we approach the van.

"Get in, get in, get *in*," The man furiously herds us into the back.

"Thanks for not leaving," River pants.

"Another ten seconds, man, and I would have," he says, pulling down the door. "Hold on to what you got. Whoa, *hello*, gorgeous." I whip my head up, and he's staring at Lily. He gives her a crooked smile, which she shakily returns.

The door secures into place, and we're locked in.

Chapter Thirty-Five

River

"Back here." I usher Delene and Lily to the containers where I hid. "Get down."

The girls hold tight to one another, and I cage them in with my body. If anything falls, it'll fall on me and not them. I gaze at Delene in awe. Yesterday, she and I had only each other, but somehow, our siblings are alive.

Adam drives with a purpose and floors it.

As the van speeds away from the lab, gunfire and shouts fade into the distance. I grab Delene's waist to steady her as the van lurches around a corner. She braces against me, shielding Lily from being tossed about in the back. Adam drives like a madman, the van bouncing roughly over the pockmarked road.

"I'm fine, Dee," says Lily, "let go so I can breathe."

Delene turns, clings to me, and buries her face against my shoulder, her body shaking. Is she crying? I brush my thumb along her wet cheek.

"Hey, it's okay. We're out. We're free." I push back her windswept hair, aching at her pain. Delene sniffs, struggling to rein in her emotions.

"I killed them, River. I took two lives, Cameron's and Dr. Lytle's." Her voice quavers.

"You did what you had to. Lytle was a monster."

Delene shakes her head, haunted. "He was still human. So much cruelty ... how could anyone become so twisted?"

I want to comfort her, to make sense of the nightmares we've faced. I brush Delene's cheek, trying to ground us both. "It's over now. We're together. That's all that matters."

Delene sighs, tension leaving her body. She presses her forehead to my chest.

"As long as I have you, I can face anything."

I pull her close, wrapping my wings around us both. We take comfort in each other's presence, spirits bruised but unbroken. Though shadows remain, the dawn will come. Together, we'll find healing.

The van jerks to a stop. I hit my head on a barrel behind me as the door opens. Adam motions frantically, "Get out *quick*."

I help Delene steady the woozy, coherent Lily. Half the Evol-humans are gone, cups and papers scattered—stragglers cluster by Glenda's office.

"Here, allow me." Adam lifts Lily, taking her to Alejandro. "Right this way, madame. Hey, Doc. Room for one more?"

"Always. Set the girl down. We'll take over from here."

I tap Alejandro on the shoulder. "How's my brother?"

"Why don't you ask him yourself?"

Porter clears a path behind two men next to Alejandro, and I grab him for a hug as Delene follows the men who tend to Lily. He looks a lot better. "I'm so glad you're alive." Okay, I'm not the most emotional of guys, but discovering your brother is still living and breathing does things to you.

"Me too."

When we part, I clamp a hand on his shoulder and search his eyes. "Are you okay?"

He pats my hand. "I'm getting there, man."

Delene and I stand before the gathered Evol-humans on the platform. I clear my throat, my pulse racing. How will they react to the news of Dr. Lytle's death?

"The lab is gone," I declare, wasting no time on pleasantries. "We destroyed it."

Chatter spreads through the gathered villagers. An Asian man with black wings etched with distinct red feathertips steps forward, suspicion evident in his eyes. "I'm Kai. What of Dr. Lytle?"

Holding Kai's gaze, I say, "Dead."

Delene steps in beside me, adding, "By my hand."

The weight of our confession presses down on me, but we need this transparency to rebuild trust and heal as a community.

A heavy silence ensues. Kai and Glenda share a brief, uneasy look. I steel myself for criticism, but hesitant cheers blossom into a full-blown celebration. I offer Delene a wry, surprised shrug. Glenda walks over, her eyes bright with emotion beneath her stern brow. As the underground Evol community leader, she's weathered decades of persecution with grit.

"Well done," she says, pride creeping into her usual no-nonsense tone. "That monster Lytle tormented our people for far too long. You've ended his bloody reign of terror."

Her hand lands reassuringly on my shoulder before she turns to face the crowd.

"Attention!" Glenda stands tall on a weathered wooden bench as we look in her direction, her eagle eyes piercing. Her arms cross her robust frame, and her feathers shift restlessly. Age lines mark her face, but her eyes burn with undiminished fire.

Our gazes lock, and she gives a slight nod, appreciating our deeds. "I don't celebrate violence, but you've ended a brutal era. The lab has been destroyed, and Dr. Lytle is gone." A cheer rises, followed by resounding applause throughout the station. Glancing back, I catch Delene's faint smile and a curious head tilt.

"Our enemies tried to break us, but we're still here. We've lost much along the way." Her eyes cloud with remembered pains. "But from the ashes, we've built a new world together."

Glenda's voice rings with passion. "Lytle is gone, but other dangers remain. As we move forward, we stay vigilant—yet *never* harden our hearts. Dark deeds cannot destroy our spirit unless we let them."

The cheering grows louder. Together, we can face the challenges ahead. I pull Delene close, and she leans against me. Though the storm intensifies, our resolve remains.

"It's time we found a new home to keep our people safe," Glenda continues. "Let them fall. Grab what you have, and let's move. Stay together. We have tents for shelter until we can build permanent homes in the forest." She hops down from the bench, in fantastic shape for her age, and approaches me. "You and Adam did an excellent job, River."

"Thank you, ma'am."

"Your grandfather would be proud."

"*Yeah*, he would," adds Porter. I may or may not have a bit of mist in my eye, but we join Delene and Lily and follow the others through the tunnels.

I read the Bible once. Pops kept small, beat-up, wallet-sized field scriptures in his cargo pants. He had us read them at night. The New Testament was more straightforward than the Old Testament, not so different from the world now.

Traveling through the tunnels reminds me of the Exodus story Pops used to have us read. No one sings or celebrates. It's a quiet victory, the air heavy with the weight of history.

Delene and I exchange glances as we walk with the others. Porter flanks my left, and in front of us, I push Lily in a wheelchair Alejandro gave us. The effects of the adrenaline shot have worn off, and she is lethargic, her head lolling to the right. A thick blanket covers her lap and legs.

"She'll be okay," I reassure Delene. "They'll take excellent care of her."

She touches my back. I glance her way. "It *will* be okay," she says, "because I have you."

To my left, Porter bobs his head, the corner of his mouth lifting. "You did good, bro. Remember when Pops told us to aim high when we found someone? I think you took that business to the next level."

The canyon trip takes twenty minutes by air but over an hour on foot. Loud shouts and rumbling echo from the streets above—something is happening.

Except for the children, everyone carries weapons. I still have the X9 strapped to my back and the handgun in my pocket. The drain's dull grates are about three hundred yards ahead. Glenda moves to her friends and stands on a cart.

"Today, we take a stand," Glenda proclaims. A burst of applause follows, but Delene, Porter, Lily, and I remain reserved, waiting to see where this leads. "For too long, we've been treated like lab rats. No more. We claim the mountains as our domain." She lifts a sign reading "Trespassers Face Death."

"We will build real homes from the earth, a village where our young can grow and fly in peace. Our days below ground are over. From now on, we're no longer Evol-humans. We're Evols."

I focus on the children in front, who feast on her words, their eyes shining with her promises. One girl stands by a cage with two chickens squawking.

A weight lifts from my heart. This could be our moment. We won't be on the run anymore. It's been so long since I've allowed myself to truly believe. Hope has felt impossible.

But I have my family, which doesn't exclusively mean Porter. I have something worth fighting for and protecting. I touch Delene's back, and she meets my eyes in the gloom, her face tightened with the emotions she's keeping tucked inside.

"This is a fresh day," Glenda calls. "Without our blood to keep them alive, humans will die. We can work something out with those who survive in the future, but today is a new day. Follow me."

The others shield their eyes from the sunlight when we lift the grated doors, but I tilt my head back, filling my lungs with fresh oxygen. *That's more like it.*

Nightfall will be here soon. In the distance, plumes of smoke and fire burn within the city walls, sending black puffs into the sky. We need to get everyone somewhere safe. I motion for Delene and Porter to wait, and I approach Glenda.

"I know where to start the village," I say.

Glenda nods. I can tell she trusts me. I pick her up and fly with her and ten others in formation to the thicket I found a week ago near the stream. I set her in the center of the large clearing surrounded by trees.

"You can see for miles from here. Plenty of game, fishing, and trapping nearby. And an apple grove we should expand."

Glenda surveys the area, hand to her heart. "It's perfect. There is enough room for homes and a good view while staying close. We'll build watchtowers by the stream." She turns to Kai. "Kai, go tell the others. Bring them here. Double up and help carry the non-fliers."

"Yes, ma'am." He flies away.

My eyes slide to the adjacent mountain. Glenda follows my gaze. "Is that where you live?"

"At the top."

"Will you join us down here, or—"

I shake my head. "I'm of more use keeping an eye out. It's where I belong."

Her lips twitch. "I thought you'd say that. You're just like your granddad."

"Thank you. I'll take that as a compliment."

"I meant it as one." She turns to inspect the grounds. "This is a fine place to settle our village. The snow will come soon, making it hard for anyone in the city to get through the mouth of the canyon. We have enough food stores to make it through winter, and we have a doctor, engineers, an architect, and you, our survival expert. Help us teach survival skills?"

I nod. "I'll teach trapping and foraging. Anything you need."

She smiles. "We'd appreciate that. And your woman, Delene?"

"She and Lily should stay in the village. But I won't be far."

Glenda steps closer and wraps me in a hug. "Thank you."

"You're welcome. Hey, I meant to ask you, what's the story with you and Pops?"

Her eyes take on a mischievous glint, and a secretive smile plays at her lips. "Well, that's a story for another time. If the world had been different, I might have been your grandmother."

I raise my eyebrows. *Wow, go Pops.* Glenda grins and puts her hands on her hips as she surveys the area. "Yes, this will do nicely. I understand you want to stay in your home, but I want you to visit daily. We have lots to discuss."

"I will," I promise. A swarm of our people flies toward us. Lily is in Porter's arms, and Delene carries the wheelchair by the handles. They land with the others, and I join them.

"They'll give us supplies and help," Delene says.

I wrap my arm around her and catch Porter's eye while he assists Lily into the wheelchair. We nod. Dusk falls, hiding the ridges. Tents and campfires shine like giant fireflies in the expanding tent village. A stack of cut tree trunks waits for building. I find comfort in the campfires. Porter sits near a fire on a log, carving a large, flat piece of wood with my knife. When we were young, he always showed his creativity by drawing or writing. Some things remain the same.

I sit beside him. "Whatcha working on, Picasso?"

"Naming this place for luck," he replies, showing the freshly carved wooden sign. "There." He turns the wooden sign to me, and inside a detailed, engraved border, in his tidy handwriting, is:

Evol Hollow

"What do you think?" He grins.

I sling my arm around his shoulders and fist-bump him with my free hand. "I think it's great, man. You haven't lost your touch."

Glenda posts guards in shifts at the mouth of the canyon, and I pull one with Porter the first night after everyone settles in while Delene spends time with Lily. The first night, there's no trouble. The humans have their hands full with whatever is happening in the city. If you fly high enough, columns of black smoke rise from the fires in the distance. Those wealthy enough to buy Evol blood will run out soon.

Back at the nest I shared with Delene—our nest, I raise the tent Glenda gave me. The EMP killer still hangs in the tree, undetected. I switch it off since the others know where I am, but it's there if needed. The soil's more solid than when we left a few days ago, and there's more snow. Lighting a fire is no longer the risk it once was, now that the soldiers won't dare come within a thousand feet of these mountains. The tent blocks the wind, is weatherproof, and sleeps six, so it has more than enough room.

I dig a gutter around the tent to prevent water and snow build-up until the cabin's built, but this will keep me much warmer. Glenda did offer me an air mattress, but I kept the one I've used—it smells like Delene.

I stand atop the plateau.

This high perch suits me, between civilization and untamed. But the people below bind me in unchartered ways I have no idea how to navigate. Up here, I'm free yet connected. Perhaps the wildest hearts still need roots to thrive. I prefer my camp, but sleeping beneath the same stars and striving together gives me purpose. I've found a home and family and will fight to protect them.

Chapter Thirty-Six

Delene

Weeks pass. I move among half-built cottages, pick up a hammer, and build. I help Glenda manage the village, take inventory, and set work schedules. Even though we sleep in tents, the beginnings of permanent buildings emerge. The speed of the construction astounds me.

I patrol the borders, on the lookout for danger. By the campfire, I watch flames consume the kindling.

Shadows undulate as I glance at our backlit tent. Through the canvas walls, Lily's outline nestles under a thick quilt in repose. Though she's healing well thanks to the doctor's care, I hover.

Her laughter mingles with Adam's gentle teasing. He's become a steady presence, attentive to her needs—refilling tea, bringing blankets, holding her hand. Tenderness fills his eyes when he looks at Lily, and she soaks it up like a sponge.

Though born without wings, Adam has proven a steadfast friend. His quick thinking helped us escape the lab. And the gentle way he looks at my sister Lily makes it clear she's stolen his heart. They've forged a special connection through loss, and sometimes, I feel like an intruder in their hushed conversations when I ask if she needs anything.

"What was your mom like?" Adam asks softly.

Lily's silhouette glances toward me, and I hear her voice crack. "She was quiet and nice, and she loved flowers. We stayed in this cabin once with wild bluebells growing in a patch on the side of the woodshed, and she would dry some and hang them in front of the door so the room smelled sweet. I think they reminded her of our grandma."

Adam chuckles. "My dad liked plants. He kept some tomato plants on our apartment balcony, and whenever I come across one, it always brings me back."

"I miss my mom," Lily whispers, and though I'm eavesdropping and it's none of my beeswax what these two lovebirds are talking about, her sad tone pains my heart.

"I know," Adam soothes. "But they're with us. They're here. And, for what it's worth, so am I."

The whisper of fabric reaches my ears. Curiosity gets the better of me, and I peek around the corner. Lily is in a tight embrace with Adam. I can't help but smile, retreating so I don't interrupt them—two souls seeking solace in each other amidst their pain. I walk away, pleased to see Lily with someone by her side. Seeing her with someone who truly values her brings warmth to my heart.

As I changed her sheets earlier today, Lily spoke in a hushed, excited tone. "Delene, I need to tell you about Adam..." A gentle blush spread across her cheeks as she recounted his kindness and their bond. Adam's unwavering support has reignited joy in Lily's life. She now shares her once-broken dreams, which are slowly coming back to life.

I wipe down the wooden tables in the chow hall and scrub the stone hearth of ashes. Trying to offer Lily and Adam some privacy, their hushed voices still drift to me, mingled with the soft crackle of the fire.

With practiced patience molded by years of leadership, Glenda draws out Kai's concerns over grain supplies. She listens without judgment and then poses thoughtful questions to guide him toward solutions. Glenda empowers others and leads by example. Her steady hand at the tiller steers us through stormy seas.

After speaking with Kai, River and I are troubled by talk of a winter food shortage. "Do you think some people will sneak into the city?" I ask. "That's risky."

River shrugs. "Desperate times call for desperate measures. The lab's destruction left the city unstable. Scavenging could be dangerous."

"There must be another way," I insist. "Maybe we could send a diplomatic envoy to request supplies?"

Shaking his head, River replies, "They'd sooner attack us than negotiate. They resent us."

I nod. "You're right. Well, let's keep thinking. We'll come up with something."

Later, I check in on Lily. Her eyes are brighter, and she has a fresh glow on her cheeks. Nighttime is different because her nightmares come. I stay with her and hold her hand, sleeping beside her, lending comfort and assuring her she's not alone. Our bond has strengthened as she heals, and she confesses she likes Adam and possibly loves him. He's a decent guy, and I'm happy for her.

I go to the chow hall in the morning to get us some food. Outside our tent, memories rush back. Faded crayon drawings on stone walls. Spinning in circles with Lily, dizzy and laughing. My parents' quiet strength and sacrifice I was too young to grasp.

Lily and Adam's laughter drifts from the tent, interrupting my daydream, and even though I'm not in there, embarrassment comes over me as if I'm an intruder, even though *he's* visiting. My lips twitch. Leave it to Lily to mix love into all of this. Of course, I'm one to talk.

Life persists, regardless of how hard things are.

As if on cue, a familiar whoosh of plumes lands behind me. "Ooh, you brought me breakfast." A breeze brushes my neck. River slides his arms around my waist and chuckles into my hair.

"Pay attention." I nuzzle my cheek against him from behind. "I'm holding food. And this isn't for you. It's for Lily."

"Adam already beat you to it. He took two plates in the tent right after you left while I waited for you on the roof."

I turn in his arms, careful of the plates. "Is that so? What's this, you keeping tabs on me now?"

"If you like. I haven't got anything better to do until things get going." With a mischievous glint, he steps forward and takes the plates. "How about we go to the nest for some alone time? I haven't had you to myself in a while."

I tuck my bottom lip in. We spend the morning together, eating breakfast and giving each other attention we haven't been able to in ages. I relish River's cuddles as the sun crests the mountains, our hearts and stomachs full. The first rays of sunrise peek behind the craggy mountains into the shadowy valley.

"I love you," I say.

He holds me closer, stroking my hair and then my healed wing. "I love you too, Delene."

We steal a blissful hour away together before returning to the village. Then, River and I part ways. He heads over to assist the men in constructing a hospital. Figuring Adam's had enough time alone with my sister, I head back to the tent.

Lily approaches, her face glowing and her hair neatly combed, but I've seen her expression a thousand times. Something's the matter.

I startle. "Lily, what are you doing out of bed?"

"Don't worry. I'm fine. Delene, *help*. Wren and Ethan are at it again. It's on the verge of turning violent."

"Seriously?" I follow her to the center of the village, exasperated. "They're *how* old?" I've been a peacemaker lately, settling disputes unexpectedly. I'm not sure how it came about, but I've found I'm diplomatic when needed, and people listen to me for whatever reason. Loud arguing cuts through my thoughts like a knife. Two Evols square off against each other, shouting, wings flapping. It'd be comical if it weren't so irritating.

Wren points at Ethan. "You messed with my water ditch, didn't you?"

"No *way*," Ethan shoots back. "Stop pointing fingers."

I step between them. "Hey, knock it off, both of you." Looking at Ethan, I say, "If you did mess with her water ditch, go fix it." To Wren, "I understand you're frustrated, but be certain you have evidence before blaming him. It could have been a raccoon or wild animal. They've come around a lot. Creating a scene in the village isn't going to resolve anything. We've got to stick together and deal with this like civil people."

They both consider me a kid who's half their age. Both cool down, and Wren says, "You're right. Sorry, Ethan." He nods.

"For what it's worth, I didn't mess with the ditch. But I'll help you fix it, okay?"

I remember Mom's words when Lily and I would argue: "Anger divides people, but compassion is the bridge." Our community needs to heal to thrive.

After resolving their quarrel, I crave solitude. Something prompts me to do this. I ask Adam to watch Lily, but it's a moot point since he's already holding his daily vigil.

When I go to the hospital construction site and mention it to River, he nods and tells me to be cautious. Love floods through me. River's protectiveness comforts me, but he gives me space, never crowding or smothering. We nurture each other's individuality—a refreshing trust. I prefer my camp, my sanctuary. But sleeping under the same stars and striving together bonds me to this community. I've found a family to fight for.

I pack food and water, and in the morning, I fly east to Colorado.

Searching through the debris and overgrown vines, I eventually locate the old place. Outside my ruined childhood bunker, I trace the faded growth chart, remembering simpler times. Sloppy crayon drawings still cling to the stone walls. I trace my finger along the lowest one with my name on it, no taller than my thigh. Was I *that* little?

Despite the world's burdens, I'm grateful for my parents' strength.

Back then, though innocent, they prepared us for the worst, even making a game of it. My mother's velvety tone echoes, reminding me, *"You have everything inside to survive this world."*

I miss you, Mom. When I close my eyes, I imagine your kind smile, your arms wrapping around me in a ghostly embrace. If only you were here now.

But she was right. The instincts, knowledge, and fighting spirit inside came from her and my dad. I didn't think as a child I'd ever be as responsible as she was or anything close to a leader. Still, when I resolved the farmland dispute earlier, there was a sensation that maybe I'd finally gotten there.

My past lingers here in this broken bunker. But my future lies in our liberated village, the life my parents dared to dream of—a life with Lily and River. I place a hand to my heart at the doorway. I'll visit again one day and maybe bring Lily and River with me to honor what our parents gave. But I'm needed. "I love you both." I secure my bag, face the dawn, and fly home.

I land in a wildflower-filled clearing on the outskirts of Evol Hollow, smiling and at peace after visiting my childhood bunker. Our village nestles between towering ridges blanketed with fragrant pine forests that echo with birdsong. The crisp mountain air fills my lungs.

A chilling scream shatters the stillness. I bolt toward the village center, my earlier contentment vanishing. Villagers cluster around the food storage shed, their faces etched with horror and outrage. River isn't among them.

I push through, pulse racing. The empty storage sacks lie like picked-over carcasses, our precious grain reserves gutted. The sheer enormity of the loss hits me, and I can't breathe. Without those food stores, we'll starve before winter's end.

Angry shouts fill the air around me as the reality sinks in for us all. Glenda stands motionless amid the ruin, her composure shattered. Kai curses in Mandarin. Someone's betrayed us in a selfish act, jeopardizing our survival. I survey the empty storage sacks scattered like discarded skins, a cold dread knotting my stomach. Kai and Glenda stand there, shell-shocked.

"Half the grain's *gone*." Kai's voice rises in disbelief. "That's enough for thirty of us. All disappeared overnight."

Thoughts tumble in my mind. How did this happen? Our food storage is a coveted part of our community, kept under lock and key. Who would, or even could, pull this off?

Glenda, usually so calm, looks grim. "Someone from our community did this," she says, her voice steady but anger evident.

Confused whispers rise from the crowd. I exchange a look with Kai, our shared understanding clear: The trust that bonded our group has been shaken deeply. Glenda's voice rings out again, "We need to talk. Everyone, meet up in the main hall."

When everyone gathers, the atmosphere tense and filled with suspicion, Glenda raises her hand for quiet. She looks tired, the day's events weighing on her.

"If the person responsible admits it," she says, her voice firm, "I promise we'll listen."

The uneasy silence finally breaks when a figure steps forward. Liz, an overly friendly, popular teen with a cherub face and curly hair, looks up with tear-filled brown eyes.

"They promised me things," she admits, shaky, "if I gave them info about us. I didn't know they'd take our food. I thought they'd *give* us some. I was trying to help."

Disbelief and confusion sweep through the crowd. Glenda fixes on Liz. "You've put us all at risk, Liz. For what? Some *promises*?"

Tears stream down Liz's cheeks, and she's devastated.

"You stupid, selfish girl. You—" Glenda stops her tirade abruptly. I turn and notice Porter's hand on Glenda's shoulder. His nostrils flare as he shakes his head, conflicted.

He speaks urgently in Glenda's ear, and I catch, "...go easy on her."

Glenda's face hardens. "Leave, Liz. Just go."

Liz's lips quiver. Her wings droop as she turns away. My heart tightens as she walks sadly across the square, her head bowed in shame.

Glenda's piercing eyes silence side conversations. Her authoritative voice compels others to listen as she outlines plans for everyone to take inventory of what food they have. Though commanding respect comes naturally to Glenda, she wields it judiciously. Her past trials taught her leadership means serving others. She builds trust through wisdom and action.

The harsh reality hits—a close friend betrayed us. Trust will be hard to come by.

I get in line for dinner after taking stock of our dwindling food with Glenda when River appears behind me.

"We've got to stop meeting like this," he says dryly. I giggle as he pecks my forehead in greeting. "Hey, you."

We fill our plates, and I tell him what happened with Liz while he worked on a building at the edge of the village. River says so much with so little as he takes it all in. He could be a chatty guy, but he's not, and I prefer it. My dad was quiet and observant, too, and I think they're the best type of men.

I settle beside River near the dying campfire, the day's revelations still weighing on us.

Unlike his usual cheerful self, Porter sits slumped and disheartened, absently shredding a leaf as he turns his thoughts inward. Losing Liz has darkened his vibrant spirit. Seeing his sadness conveys his depth of feeling more than words can. He takes a deep breath.

"I can't believe Liz did this," he says, shaking his head.

River nods as he absorbs the situation's gravity. "We're all having a hard time accepting it."

Porter hesitates, then blurts, "I had a crush on her. Liz. Sounds foolish, right? We worked together in the crops. I thought she was so cute and funny. And she always laughed at my jokes. I was on the verge of asking her out."

I glance at River. What are his thoughts on this? But River remains contemplative and considers his words, "Emotions come and go, P. They don't have to make sense."

Porter grins wryly. "Always the deep philosopher, aren't you, Riv? It was nothing but a passing attraction with Liz—no big deal. Still, finding who she truly was? That twists the knife deep."

I squeeze Porter's hand in sympathy. "We never saw Liz's betrayal coming. I didn't know her well, but she always acted nicely."

A mischievous gleam enters Porter's eyes as his grin returns. "Guess this proves you can't judge a book by its cover ... especially a mystery novel. There's always a twist." His laugh rings out as he tries to lift our spirits.

River smirks and plays along with his twin's humor. "Oh yeah. Top-notch judgment right there."

I laugh, too, but Porter's smile fades. He grows serious. "It may have been nothing between us, but the whole thing makes me sick."

I tilt my head and give Porter a sympathetic grin. "We've all had memories we regret. They're part of growing up and learning hard lessons. None of us could have predicted what Liz did. Trust me, when it's right with someone"—I look at River—"you'll know." River puts his arm around me and pulls me close.

The three of us sit quietly, united by our unspoken bond. For now, it's enough.

Once Porter bids us goodnight, River turns to me. "Did you find what you were looking for in Colorado?"

At peace, I smile. "I did. I'm good."

He smiles back with his eyes, lifts my hand, and kisses my knuckles. "Come back to my camp."

"Okay."

The next day, Glenda beckons me to walk with her. "Yesterday was one-fourth of our problems," she mutters, trudging through the village in her boots. She's been in a foul mood since the Liz Incident. She leads me to the crop fields outside the village. I cover my mouth as I take it all in.

The morning sun shows the full extent of the devastation—rows and rows of shriveled, blackened crops stretch the fields that once buzzed with life. The Blight has taken everything from us.

I look over the withered remains, bitterness rising in my throat. My careful nurturing and optimism are gone in a cruel instant. My fellow Evols stand beside me.

"What do we *do*?" someone voices our despair.

Alejandro bends down next to us, letting the dead soil slip through his fingers. "The Blight drained the life from the earth. Nothing will grow."

"Could we find enough wild plants to make up for it?" Lily offers sadly.

Glenda shakes her head, looking burned out. "It's the same everywhere in the valley. With the snow getting heavier, even the animals are going hungry."

The harsh reality hits me. Without those fields, our food reserves drain. River takes a group up the canyon to hunt, and they bring back a deer, which helps. The hype fades, replaced with the question everyone silently asks: where will our next meal come from?

Once we ration, the idea of the hollow eyes and gaunt faces of the children haunts me. Some venture beyond the village, hoping to find anything to eat. But there's not enough. River's as frustrated as I am, but he's patient. He knows how to be hungry. One morning, he takes Porter and me to the bunker they discovered a year ago, which still has a few cases of MREs. We bring them to the village and ration everything to the last jam packet. We spread the food over a few days with fifty-plus people and twenty-four MREs.

By week's end, the first group leaves to raid. Knowing their desperation, I offer advice on where to look.

With every scanty meal, dread grows inside me—the horror of my community fading and starving after all we've achieved and fought for. I consider the previously unthinkable, my hands shaking. Maybe it's time to venture back into the city.

I help Glenda assess the damage.

Screams shatter the peaceful morning. I rush to the horrified crowd, finding a bloodied Liz with a giant bear standing over her. River sprints past, knife in hand. He jumps on the bear, driving the blade deep. After a harrowing struggle, the bear falls. Despite his bravery, sadness fills River's eyes—he doesn't harm animals lightly.

I approach Liz, assessing wounds far too severe for a bandage. She's still breathing. River scoops her up, and we hurry to the doctor, but he can't save her despite his efforts. Grief grips Evol Hollow. This deep, painful loss is one of countless trials since founding our village.

By the fire, discussions about security heat up. Some suggest walls, others alarms. River, lost in mourning, remains silent. Finally, he speaks. "We won't lock ourselves away," he asserts, "but we must take steps to prevent future tragedies."

I soothe him, stroking his neck. Catching movement in the window, I tap River's shoulder. "It's Porter."

River gets to his feet beside me. "Where?" Porter had stayed away while the doctor tried to save Liz's life.

I take his hand. "Come on."

We spot Porter sitting alone outside the village perimeter, aimlessly whittling at a branch. He doesn't even glance up when we approach. Still, his unmistakable heaviness tells me he's aware.

River steps forward, his voice tentative. "Hey, got room for one more over there?"

I hang back as Porter shrugs, the knife in his hand continuing its meticulous work on the bark. River cautiously takes a seat on a boulder beside him. The quiet between them stretches, only interrupted by the mountain gust rustling through the pines.

"You doing okay?" River asks.

Pain flashes across Porter's face, and he sets aside the half-stripped branch he was working on. "Liz was..." His voice wavers as he admits, "I liked her. Okay, more than liked. I downplayed it, but I kissed her."

River's eyebrows lift as he leans closer. "You did? When?"

"Yesterday. Before the meeting. It doesn't matter. Now Liz is gone. For no reason."

Even from afar, their conversation weighs heavy. River places a hand on Porter's shoulder. "I know," he intones, his voice laced with pain. "It's senseless."

"I should have stopped Glenda from sending her away. I should have—"

River's voice cracks as he echoes Porter's grief. "There was nothing you could have done, P. She did what she did, and she had to leave. None of it was your fault."

"Then why does it hurt so much?" Porter's shoulders tremble. "It could've been any of us. One wrong move..."

"You're right," River agrees, his voice low. "We're not safe, not even here." He searches Porter's eyes, and I see him willing to give all the support he can. "But we have each other. And we're taking steps to protect our home. Liz's loss won't be in vain."

They sit side-by-side, the setting sun casting its orange glow on them. As the night descends, fireflies appear, their pleasant twinkling offering a brief distraction from the pain. Even if words fall short, River's hand on Porter's shoulder provides comfort. I'm grateful River is there for his brother in such a critical moment.

I check on Lily's recovery to keep busy and useful. I volunteer to patrol the perimeter.

Lily grows stronger by the day. Though proud of our village, my heart yearns for River. I fly up the cliff in my downtime to be alone with him. We lounge by the fire beneath the stars, blankets draped over us, simply existing together without fear for our survival. It's nice.

River sweeps my hair aside, kissing my neck as I doze. "Stay here with me." Hand-in-hand, I snuggle closer. This hidden world is ours. We return to it and each other whenever we can.

By the week's end, we beef up the village security with wooden palisades and set up traps. Even though we can't undo what happened, we ensure Liz's loss will help keep others safe.

Chapter Thirty-Seven

River

For weeks, the food shortage plagues every home. Children's ribs show through thin shirts. We work from dawn till dusk constructing wattle-and-daub shelters despite our hunger. Each small step brings us closer. We can't afford to surrender—too much depends on our grit.

Under the warm sun, I weave dried grass into insulation boards. As a descendant of Aztec and Native American ancestors, Glenda possesses invaluable knowledge of their architectural techniques. Her expertise guides the construction of longhouses in the village, echoing building methods from generations past.

Evols weave everywhere—on rooftops, laying bricks. Around me, the others work diligently and chat as they turn mud and straw into sturdy buildings. After being alone, my fondness for those around me grew, though it took time. I finally belong.

Where this land was once a broad field, our village now transforms the valley. Neat wooden cottages send up fingers of smoke. I'm amazed at what we've accomplished.

Laughter floats up from around crackling cooking fires. The last dusty orange rays of the setting sun bathe the fertile fields of swaying green crops surrounding the village, everything aglow in the warm light.

After so much hardship, witnessing this community thrive gives me strength.

As kids, we constantly moved. "Don't get attached," Pops warned. I lived a solitary existence, isolated from connections until Delene came along and opened my eyes.

Though life's uncertain, we weather storms together. I'm still wild at heart, but not alone. These people give me purpose.

The raiding party returns with canned goods, improving our food stores—Kai's team plants vegetable beds where seedlings already sprout. I plan to take a team to collect bees from a beehive and appoint a beekeeper for homemade honey. Despite our crop issues, I encourage others not to give up hope.

When it boils down to it, I've been through a lot worse and learned everything in life is about your perspective. If you think you have it hard, you do. If you feel like rough times will never end, they won't. It's about moving forward despite the setbacks and driving on no matter what.

The longhouses loom over the village center, golden-hay roofs glowing in the fading light. Intricately carved poles prop up woven, mud-plastered walls. Inside, women sew quilts as children race around, oblivious to elders' scoldings. Men whittle toys and tools at a long table, rounding edges and sanding smooth. The scents of fresh-cut timber and burning hickory from the great stone hearth fill the air.

Outside the longhouse doors, riders on horseback trot down the main village road, bundles of grain and bales of hay balanced carefully behind their saddles. Between the wooden cottages, women with fluttering wings chat as they hang laundry in the sun.

The rhythmic clank of tools blends with the hum of salvaged motors by the river's edge. Our engineers have rekindled old wind turbines and water wheels for power. Despite their age, the gears and levers chatter and spin, a testament to Evol ingenuity.

Villagers, their hands stained with mud and wood shavings, heave large planks into place. Voices, interspersed with laughter and concentration, shout over the din, coordinating their efforts as the silhouette of a water wheel takes shape. Children run between them, reconstituting the boundaries of an old hopscotch grid etched into the dirt, as oblivious to hardship as only the young can be. Their giggles and shouts fill the warm afternoon.

As I take in all these sights—the orderly cottages sending up wisps of smoke, chatter, and children laughing, wings fluttering—a deep sense of belonging warms me. After a lifetime of isolation, constantly moving from place to place, this feels like home.

With each new build, we improve—Pops would see a metaphor here.

Kai read what he could about farming, and Glenda gave solid building advice. However, there's much to learn about building a community from scratch. Young, orderly rows of crops ripple on the village's western side, and some older Evols with engineering backgrounds dug irrigation trenches from the nearby stream to guide water and fertilize the soil.

The longhouses double as a chow hall, classroom, and sewing workshop. I smile from the doorway as Lily reads to a circle of young Evols. With a warmth that reaches her eyes, Lily smiles at her students as they finish their lessons and run off to play. Despite enduring immense cruelty, she nurtures the next generation with gentle wisdom.

As I turn to leave, Glenda emerges from the other longhouse, a mouthwatering aroma of stew trailing behind. We exchange nods. My respect for her grows daily. She's taught us ancestral cooking over open fires. I would have eaten well on the run if I had known half of those skills.

People make life better, I admit.

Later that night, weary and fulfilled, I head to the chow hall, where Delene waits with a plate. We eat together in comfortable silence before the meeting. We're both on the council, and the sessions run late into the night as we navigate self-governance. Evol Hollow is in its infancy, but with guts and resolve, anything is possible.

A few months after we get settled in, I offer to make a reconnaissance flight with other council members and survey what's left of the city.

We fly in formation, lower than I usually would alone. There's no real need for concealment because the humans have little left. People look up at us as we pass, but in the aftermath of the revolution, crowds swarm the streets, protesting or pleading, I can't tell which. Their ravaged bodies look sickly, pale, and gray. Their cries are clear, and my heart sympathizes despite what we've been through. No one wanted this, any of this.

The lab lies in rubble, a consequence of their cruelty. Now, *humans* face turmoil.

The crowd stands around the ruins, waving tattered cardboard signs of anger and despair.

As we fly over, their pleading grows. Some extend desperate arms, begging for rescue. *We're sorry,* they shout, *help us, please*!

The five of us land on a high rooftop, staring at the desperation around us.

Makeshift tents parody our early village—heated debates and mad gestures directed our way. They want our blood and are discussing it like it's normal, and while we're brave in coming here, I don't dare stay. Delene waits for me back in the village.

Desperation drives people to do unthinkable things.

I swallow and look over my shoulder. "I've seen enough. Let's go back." The others nod.

I soar, my stomach churning. The weight of our actions will haunt me, though destroying the lab was right. This is the steep price of freedom.

Back in the village, we call a council meeting. I stand and deliver our report that humans pose no real threat to us. Caught off guard, I meet Delene's solemn gaze across the table. Her expression shifts, brows furrowed in concern. I shake my head and look away.

I'd help the humans if I could save one or more people and donate blood. But their situation is out of our hands. We have a bigger problem to deal with.

Glenda and Lily are three steps ahead as they get locked in a heated discussion to determine what we do from here. Lily wants peace with the humans. She's healed and every bit Delene's sister as she speaks her mind and argues passionately. Glenda is adamant we stay isolated and let nature run its course. And because she is our de facto leader, everyone listens to her.

Alejandro drafts a list of basic rules for governance for Evol Hollow, which sparks a huge debate. Everyone offers their two cents. I stay quiet, the images of the dying, desperate humans so real in my mind they might as well be in front of me.

Kai and Alejandro lock horns over water rations and how much to direct into the village, which Glenda diffuses calmly. People listen to her, and she's a good leader. The meeting is about to end.

I stand among the villagers as Glenda climbs onto a crate, capturing everyone's attention. She lifts her hand, and a hush falls over the square.

"Friends, this has been a challenging period. Threats lurked in the shadows, endangering our village."

A buzz of agreement ripples through the gathered crowd. Glenda's attention rakes over the Evols who had recently emerged from the tunnels, their posture upright, confident, and safe.

"When the danger loomed, threatening our very existence, we were at a loss," Glenda continues, her eyes finding mine. "One of us courageously fought, leading the Evols to safety and guiding their adaptation for survival."

All eyes focus on me, standing in my worn jacket, evidence of recent adventures still clinging to it. I glance at Delene, but she grins and touches my arm.

"Because of your dedication, River, these beings survive *and* thrive. You didn't merely lead them out of those tunnels. You gave them a new lease on life and a better future." A mix of embarrassment and pride swamps me as Glenda beckons me over. As I walk to her, she grips my shoulder with gratitude. "Your brave deeds are a testament to what we aim to be, individually and as a village. May your courage be our guiding light."

Applause and cheers surround me. Many pat my back, speaking grateful words. I accept their praise, humbled and warmed more by Glenda's recognition than any fire.

"Thanks," I whisper to Glenda as the crowd disperses. "But I did what I did for Delene and Porter. And without your guidance, we'd have lost so much more."

She gives my shoulder a comforting pat. "Let's discuss more over warm food."

Together, we walk in peaceful silence. The village buzzes back to life around us with hope in every step.

Later, a mouthwatering fresh bread aroma draws me back from hunting. I follow the heavenly scent to the chow hall, where Delene expertly braids loaves to bake in the communal oven. I discovered a while ago that she has a knack for braids, and I even let her plait weaves in my hair one night.

"The Jill of all trades, huh?" I lean against the wall, amazed. *Is there anything this woman can't do?*

"You better believe it," she sasses.

Her clever hands weave the golden dough with grace, slender fingers dancing and looping as she crafts an edible work of art. I pause in the doorway, transfixed.

My stomach rumbles, a traitor to my hunger. Delene looks up and laughs, warming me like a fire-heated oven.

"Patience," she chides playfully. "This batch needs a bit longer to rise."

I run a hand through my hair. But the cracker-like, warm, malty aromas from the kitchen are impossible to resist.

Delene wipes her flour-dusted hands and comes close, her hair tucked back neatly into a ponytail, a few stray wisps loose. I push them back, fingertips grazing her cheek.

"Tell you what." Her eyes dance with delight. "You get the first warm loaf from the oven."

I grin, anticipation rising. "Lucky me. Mind if I wait? Don't want to miss that first buttery bite."

Delene swats my shoulder, her lilting laughter music to my ears. I settle onto a nearby stool, content. Watching her bake fills me with simple joy. She feeds more than my appetite.

Soon, I'll savor the bread. But I'll happily steal these small pockets of time together. This is home.

By week's end, the village takes concrete shape—orderly rows of longhouses, cabins, barns. Delene and Lily now have a house where their tent stood. I visit daily, though we've both been busy. She teaches the children to read, and people gravitate to her.

Evol Hollow is becoming a community, with everyone working side-by-side to build houses, prepare food for winter, and help one another.

Losing people hurts deeply, but the pain's worth the connections. Working alongside my neighbors and sharing dreams and burdens, I feel a sense of belonging I've never known before.

A hunting party returns with a few deer, and we gather in the chow hall. Delene sits beside me, quiet as she chews her venison stew and watches the flamelight. I've given her space since she returned from Colorado. She confided in me why she went, and I got it.

Chapter Thirty-Seven

I will never admit this, but the nest is cold without her.

Glenda thumps the table, and the room falls silent. She stands, surveying us all. "With the lab destroyed and reports of the humans' fate, the power they took from us long ago has been restored."

Silence meets her speech. I avoid her eyes, haunted by images of dying people. What wisdom could I offer after what I witnessed?

Glenda raises her voice. "So, the next step is crucial as we decide how we harness that power."

Lily pushes to make peace, but Glenda refuses, insisting humans are now monsters. Adam and Alejandro object, arguing we shouldn't stoop to their level. A heated debate ensues as many voices chime in. I reflect on the desperate humans lost in the darkness of fear.

"River?"

I turn to Delene, who has questions in her eyes. "What do you think about all this?"

What do I think? I think of Pops and how he believed a person's last drop of integrity mattered. I think about how he spoke of empathy and compassion, my parents' sacrifice, and of Porter, Delene, and Lily. I touch Delene's back as I stand and clear my throat.

"I'll tell you what I think," I make my voice clear and loud, like Pops. The room turns its attention to me. I take her hand and lead her to the front next to Glenda. She offers me a light squeeze.

"My grandfather had a saying. Violence breeds violence," I say, meeting each council member's eyes. "We must take the first step toward peace through mercy. If not now, then soon."

Delene stands tall beside me as if she's proud. People break into furious undertones. I need this to hit home because people are dying while we're comfortable and situated. They have to listen because the last thing we need is more destruction.

Our council meeting lasts through the night. Around the fire, twenty of us discuss democracy. I never thought I'd be a politician, but here I am.

Arguments fly, and groups form. Some want a strong leader for stability. No one denies Glenda's perfect for the job as she runs the place anyway, but some have objections about how we handle it.

"We don't need another dictator," Lily counters. We decide power should be shared by all.

Glenda listens intently, her sharp eyes shifting between speakers. "You make fair points," she concedes. "But without structure, we'll fail. Let's compromise and lay ground rules." She has a knack for mediating and guiding us to common ground.

I think of our past and decide to speak up. "No flying restrictions. No forced labor."

Delene adds, "Or limits on love." People nod. Everyone's on board.

We discuss until dawn, creating rules for everyone's safety. While not everyone agrees, we find a compromise, bringing order and unity to the group.

By morning, we implement our rules and gather around the charter. Not perfect, but it's a start. I sign my signature, sensing Pops nearby, proud and boasting. We're building a new world.

It's a long journey, but we're in it together—one step at a time.

I'd have laughed a year ago at patiently teaching a dozen Evol children. But here I am. The children gather around, eyes wide with curiosity.

Little Iris asks, "What are we learning today, Uncle River?"

I hold up my knife. "I'm going to teach you how to build a snare trap, an important survival skill."

With practiced hands, I weave the supple willow branches into a snare, cinching the slip knot tight. I explain how to blend the snare into the surroundings, scattering leaves and sticks to disguise it. The children watch my every move, their bright eyes reflecting the firelight.

As Pops once taught me, sensing his wisdom, I pass tolerance to the children.

"The most important thing is patience," I say. "It takes time to master skills. But practice, and you'll provide food for your families one day."

Their tiny faces bloom with pride. A pang of sadness hits me, too, realizing these children have the chance at a childhood Pops tried so hard to give us. Their eager minds ignite a flame of hope. If we guide the next generation, a brighter future awaits.

I end the lesson and put some work in on my cabin.

A soft wind blows through the pines as I lock the final log, completing the cabin's roof. I inhale the fresh, crisp air, enjoying the fruity overtones.

I stand back, admiring my handiwork. The sturdy walls. The sloped ceiling. I built this cabin by hand, tucked against soaring mountain walls with rustling pines. I chose this hidden retreat for Delene and me to share our life.

Community sounds drift up from below—children laughing, axes chopping. Nature's voice up here, how I want it.

When Glenda asked me to stay in the village, I hesitated. The mountains are in my blood. Confined walls make me restless. But to never visit those I've come to care for? Unthinkable.

So, I compromised by building this cabin, nestled between civilization and the untamed wild. Close enough to see the village lights twinkle at night, I'm not far. But the remoteness provides the solitude I crave.

Pops would shake his head and call me a stubborn fool. "You don't need to do everything alone, son," he'd say. And he'd be right. I don't, not anymore. But old habits die hard.

I've gotten closer to Glenda, who occasionally appears to share surprising Pops stories. As I stand by the edge of the cabin, Glenda's revelation about her past with Pops plays in my mind. The thought of the two of them, young and in love amidst top-secret trials, choosing duty over personal desires, is still a lot to digest.

Their affair happened before he met my grandma, of course. Still, he and Glenda escaped with promises to return, promises that Glenda held onto, even decades later. With every story she shares, I realize we built our village with wood, stone, *and* tales of undying love and resilience. There's comfort in knowing Pops is here. It's a more complex and richer history than I ever imagined.

As I watch from a rooftop, the setting sun casts the village in a coral hue. Children's laughter rises from the square, mingled with the scent of fresh bread. My gaze settles on the sign: *Evol Hollow*, our haven built on community. Once, I believed in solitude, thinking strength meant walking alone.

Experiencing loss made me wary, so I adopted a mantra of self-preservation. But Delene changed that. She cracked my hardened heart, painting my world with purpose and joy.

Below, I see her with Lily, their wings touching in sisterly love. Porter, my once-lost brother, returned to me, adding to our growing kinship circle. Here, among misfits, we flourish. And as I teach the Evol children, their eager eyes fuel my renewed sense of purpose. As the first glimmers of stars peek out, I recall nights alone under boundless skies, disconnected and adrift. Now, love and purpose anchor me. Darkness endures in this imperfect world, but Delene lights my way as we walk together.

As I stock the cabin with hand-carved furniture and winter provisions, I imagine Delene by the fire, wrapped in blankets.

I paint the cabin's walls, picturing her smile lighting up the small space. It's interesting how my plans for solitude shifted to include someone else. But some roots naturally entwine.

Several weeks after building the cabin, I stand in the doorway, gazing at the sun-kissed valley. This cabin suits me, but it could shelter two. I'll craft a bookshelf next, I decide. And have the chimney smoke ready to greet Delene when she flies over. My place, but no longer mine. Our place. A new beginning.

I go to the village for supplies, and a breeze brushes my neck. Delene lands beside me, radiant, golden hair spilling over her shoulders.

"Moving up in the world, huh?"

I set my box of supplies down as she nestles into my arms. "I missed you," I murmur, breathing her sweet scent.

She describes life in the village as I take her hand and lead her through the mountains. We approach the secluded home I built, nestled against soaring walls and pines. Delene grasps my hand, marveling at the log cabin's sloping roofline and the wisp of smoke coiling from the stone chimney.

I've carved a wooden table, two hand-hewn chairs, and a frame for the bed we'll share. Delene runs her hand over the smooth grain of the table, eyes shining. She turns in a slow circle, taking in the panoramic mountain view framed through the wide window over the kitchen sink.

"Oh, River, it's *perfect*." She traces the weathered grain, taking in every detail of the hand-carved table. I play it cool but bristle with pride. This is for her. All for her.

Two hooks above the fireplace await our jackets. I hang mine and drape Delene's over the other. In the golden firelight, they overlap like two pieces fitted together, like us.

"How are you doing down in Evol Hollow?"

"Good, though it's weird with you gone."

"You miss my snoring, huh?"

"Exactly."

"Well, we're together *now*."

She sighs. "It's not the same, though. I miss the closeness. Lily likes being near Adam and everyone. It gives her a sense of safety. How's Porter?"

I kiss the top of her head. "He's good. He's off hunting and checking the snares I set a few days ago. Should be back soon."

"Think Porter can find those snares?"

"Are you kidding? Pops trained us to track anyone. He's a bloodhound." I point to the cabin's outline. "I'll build two floors—living space and a full kitchen."

"Well, *you've* got it under control."

"That I do. Is Lily okay?" Every time her sister comes into view, she looks haunted, as though she could break if someone snaps their fingers. It's not like I could blame her. If a psychopath had surgically taken my wings and left me incapacitated on a gurney, I'd be a mess, too.

Delene nods. "She's on edge, which is understandable. But she's warmed up to Adam. I believe they're growing fond of each other."

There's no mistaking her innuendo. I pull away to read her expression and stroke her upper back. "Really?"

"Mmhmm. He has a soft spot for her. He always comes by, ensuring we have enough food and extra supplies. Hey, I'm not going to complain. She's never had a boyfriend so attentive, and it helps."

I lift my eyebrows. "Well, you know, Adam's a good guy. And if it frees you up so we can spend more time together, I'm all for it."

"Me too."

I wrap my arms around her. "Welcome home."

Chapter Thirty-Eight

Delene

One Year Later

The fiddle's music surrounds me as River takes my hand, leading me into a dance. Evol Hollow pulses with the cheer of the first Harvest Festival—laughter and clinking cups echoing as villagers feast and children nibble sweets. Lanterns glow above, strings crisscrossing building to building. River's hand rests between my wings as we move together, steps merging. I look into his eyes, my heart swelling with love.

This valley was barren a year ago, but we've turned it into a fruitful haven. I inhale the aromas of honeyed squash, tomatoes, tangy apples, and hay. Our full barns and storerooms prove the thriving community we've built.

As the fiddle's melody crescendos, Evols whirl around us, some even dancing mid-air. Amidst the dance, River dips me, filling me with pride and wonder. He pulls me close when the music ends as we sway beneath the lantern-lit canopy. We've forged a thriving village from the ashes of the past, hidden here in this valley between the mountains. Many challenges loom in the outside world. Still, we've built a refuge of joy, family, and freedom within Evol Hollow's wooden walls.

The harvest moon hangs full and bright as we stroll hand-in-hand along the riverbank, leaving the laughter and music of the village feast behind. There is no need for words when we're this close.

I pause to face River, taking both his hands in mine. "Do you remember the morning we first met, when you found me in your nest?"

River chuckles. "How could I forget? A mysterious, gorgeous, injured girl appears out of nowhere, invading my privacy."

His eyes dance playfully. "You turned my whole world upside down."

"For the better?"

River caresses my cheek, smiling tenderly. "For the *best*. You gave my life meaning. You amaze me, Delene." His voice grows husky with emotion. "Loving you is the best thing that ever happened to me."

Joy wells up inside me, mirroring his. "And you've shown me the world through new eyes, River. I can't imagine life without you."

He pulls me close. "You won't have to. We're in this together."

"Through whatever comes," I vow.

River seals our promise with a kiss, conveying the unspoken. We turn hand-in-hand, following the river home, where our dreams await. Though our past haunts us, River and I have a strong bond guiding us forward. Our hearts are united, and we'll face any challenge together.

December, one month later

At first, snowflakes drift down gently as River leaves to hunt. But soon, an unforgiving blizzard rages, with ferocious winds and plummeting temperatures. Villagers rush indoors, stoking fires for warmth. Some remain outside, desperately shielding livestock and buildings from the storm.

I'm among those helping to board up windows and secure anything threatened by the storm. The cold bites harder and nips at my feathers, penetrating my jacket.

I've witnessed many storms, but nothing like this. Over the field, I barely recognize Glenda's figure, her shouts of instruction almost lost in the roaring gusts. We secure a few things as the world turns white, erasing visibility. Glenda's voice cuts through one last time: "Take cover." The wind greedily snatches her words away, making them even harder to decipher.

I find solace by the fire inside our snow-bound cabin while worrying for River and tending to feverish Lily. My positivity wanes as the relentless blizzard rages for days, but a change comes on the third day.

The storm recedes, revealing a world blanketed in untouched, gleaming snow. The village comes alive as everyone assesses the damage and digs out. I help distribute supplies, ensuring those most in need get them. The storm tried to break us but instead revealed our community's strength and compassion.

When River returns, I rush into his arms, weak with relief, kissing him madly. Surveying the damage, we share somber acceptance. This storm tested our people's spirit, but we remain unbroken.

A week after the blizzard battered Evol Hollow, I survey the destruction as dawn breaks—caved roofs, collapsed walls, trees strewn like matchsticks. I'm overwhelmed by the monumental tasks ahead. Where do we even begin?

But as the sun rises higher, the villagers emerge from their shelters, shoulders set with determination. Kai organizes work crews, dispatching teams to clear roads and haul lumber. "We'll have this place shipshape before long," he declares.

I join a roof repair crew with River, Adam, and Porter. We remove damaged sections before nailing new timber supports and thatching the holes. River's solid and steady hands guide me on the tasks. Despite the exhaustion from hours of labor, seeing the solid new roof take shape rekindles my spirit.

By the river, Lily and Glenda oversee a communal greenhouse promising fresh vegetables soon, their optimism boosting morale.

In the evenings, we gather around fires, sharing stews. The children's laughter as they race around lifts our spirits.

During the long nights, we craft to pass the time until sleep takes over—whittling, weaving, sewing. With a shy smile, Porter presents a superbly carved wooden doll to little Iris. Iris's green eyes dance with pure delight as she cradles the doll. Though overshadowed by his twin, Porter has a gentle, fun soul and clever woodworking hands like Pops. The children adore his handcrafted toys.

I piece quilts together, each stitch meditating hope.

Signs of recovery quickly sprout across the village. Though deep snow smothers the fields, buildings stand strong, floors bustling. Much work remains, but unified in purpose, we'll make it through.

It's been one month since the blizzard, and spring's first shoots peek through the receding snow. Today, the timber schoolhouse frame stands ready for raising. River clasps my shoulder, pride in his eyes.

"We did this together," he says in awe. I lean into him, heart swelling, knowing nothing defeats the human spirit. As I bask in the warm sunlight, determination fills me. We'll rebuild, even with challenges ahead.

Later, our fireplace's glow fills the cabin, sheltering us with memories—the leaning bookshelf brimming with tales, the oak table holding echoes of meals shared. The fireplace, made of collected stones, warms us alongside cushions, inviting closeness. Small windows balance privacy and openness. Each corner captures our once unimaginable bond. I can't fathom life without River or this sanctuary we've built together. He snaps me from my thoughts as he hands me tea.

"Thinking about Lily's wedding?" he asks, chuckling.

"Yes. Lily's set on having the ceremony by the waterfall, where mist and sunlight create rainbows. Since we came here, she's always loved that place. It's magical." Lily has embraced whimsy and beauty despite the darkness she endured.

"Sounds wet. But sure, magical."

I scoff and trace patterns on his hand when he pulls me close. "We're free now," I say. "The shadows are gone. It's a new world without monsters."

He tightens his hold, his voice brimming with emotion. "The monsters are history. We have our future. We could even have a family someday."

My heart flutters, "Have you ... considered children?"

"All the time," he confesses. "But only with you."

I gasp. River's next move surprises me even more.

He kneels and produces a small, carved wooden box showing off a ring fashioned from vines and a diamond. "Delene," River says, his voice filled with sincerity, "I'm no poet, but I love you. Will you marry me?"

Tears blur my vision as I kneel and embrace him, "Yes, River. Forever."

He places the ring on my finger, a perfect fit. "To clean slates," he kisses my forehead.

"And dreams realized," I add, resting my head on his sturdy shoulder.

Six months later

Six months after becoming an engaged woman, I deftly weave Lily's long copper hair into an intricate braid suitable for her wedding day. As she sits before the cracked mirror in our cottage, we chat and giggle, immersed in memories from our childhood. It's hard to believe we're here, free to celebrate love and family after everything we endured. But we persevered and built a new life.

"Remember when we snuck those chocolates from the rations?" Lily asks between giggles. "Mom was so mad. She called them her PMS chocolates."

I chuckle, remembering. "Or when we belted out songs past bedtime? It's a wonder our parents were sane."

As we laugh together, our shared memories flow—adventures in abandoned buildings, scaling rocky cliffs with our dad, skimming stones on serene lakes, and learning to fly— simpler times.

I secure the braid's end with a faded strip of cloth, frayed at its edges. Our mother once used this very strip to tie back our hair when we were young. I found it at the bunker, and the familiar fabric carries echoes of her kind, caring hands.

I hold up a mirror, admiring my work. Lily turns her head, cascades of copper rippling down her back in the intricate plait. She looks like she did when we played those childhood games—eyes bright with spirit, glowing with joy, but she's a woman now.

We both are.

I love my sister deeply. In this world of constant change, we've stayed together. Today, she'll take brave steps toward her future. I'll be by her side, bound by unforgettable memories. I check her dress and hair one last time.

"It's perfect." Lily pulls me into a fierce embrace. And in her arms, I'm grateful beyond words.

Lily and Adam's wedding day is full of magic. They dance joyfully, and my sister glows, wreathed in bridal flowers. After all she endured, who could have imagined this?

Yet here we stand, honored guests at the village's first wedding. I grow emotional at my radiant sister's billowing lace gown.

Adam gazes at her with a lifetime's worth of naked adoration.

As they dance, Adam whispers to Lily. Eagerly, she nods as he presses a remote control, unveiling the intricate mechanical wings he crafted for her. Coos of awe ripple through the crowd. Lily takes a deep breath and steadies herself. Then, she leaps into the air, her powerful mechanical wings beating to the music's rhythm. She ascends gracefully over the grass, elegantly spiraling through the sunlit air. I blink back tears of wonder and pride at my sister flying again.

Around me, the villagers whoop and cheer Lily on, hands raised toward the sky. She loops happily across the treetops, dancing in the wind. As she descends, Adam stretches out his arms. Lily lands in his embrace, bio-mechanical feathers folding behind her. So *that's* what he did all those months we planned the wedding. And here, I thought he was just lazy. I smirk at my brother-in-law, who gives me a cheeky wink and shrug.

They come together in a tender kiss, and I cheer the loudest. Today, we celebrate Lily finding a loving partner and the unity of our community. The darkness won't reclaim us. I won't allow it. Joy awaits. Today is only the start.

My heart warms — Adam is Lily's once-in-a-lifetime love.

"Hey, honey, look." I tap River's shoulder, pointing to a cluster of downy feathers where a dozen village children eagerly watch Porter shaping a fallen oak branch into a spinning top. Their gasps and giggles fill the air as Porter hands a freshly carved top to a young boy, delight dancing in the child's eyes. Porter ruffles his hair affectionately before selecting another branch.

I remember River telling me stories. Since boyhood, he and Porter loved to carve wood, as Pops had taught them. They would sit for hours by the fire as his experienced, worn hands crafted simple playthings from scraps.

Porter patiently teaches young Timothy to cast a fishing line at the stream's edge. His calm encouragement gives Timothy the confidence to keep trying when his line gets snagged on a rock. Porter's a born mentor, guiding others with empathy earned through his trials. His inner light touches those around him.

Our eyes meet. Porter's are peaceful as he bridges his past with the future. Pride swells within me, seeing Porter pass on

Pops's whittling skills to the children, bonding generations. Porter delights the children with an easy grin and makes silly faces as he whittles. His youthful spirit effortlessly connects with theirs. Carving the toys brings Porter joy too—it links him to grandfatherly wisdom passed down through generations.

The children hold tight to their new toys, filled with pure adoration, as they look up at him. Perhaps Porter has found a new calling.

"May I have this dance?" River extends his hand, eyes twinkling. My engagement ring sparkles in the sun, and I laugh, joining him under the sunlit canopy where villagers whirl across grass and air.

Our wings skim as we turn gracefully to the music.

As we dance, tears of joy fill my eyes. River dispels the shadows. Our friendship became a partnership—he's my world now. I lean into him as we slow, thankful. Here we stand, surrounded by those we love, on land we've tilled and built with our hands. This village is where our vision came to life.

River's chin grazes my hair. "Are you happy?"

"With you and Lily, I'm happier than ever."

I look up, and River's mouth lifts in a crooked grin. He kisses me tenderly.

Together, we've created a haven, though shadows loom elsewhere. As long as we hold onto love and each other, I believe we can make the light spread.

This blissful day is only the beginning.

One year later

One year after Lily and Adam's joyous wedding celebration in Evol Hollow, I hold River's hand tightly as we enter the human city, flanked on all sides by our winged kin. We've worked hard to build this bridge between us. Despite past wounds, today, we arrive in peace, offering aid. There's still room for understanding, for a brighter bond.

The once-lifeless streets now pulse with energy beneath solar lights.

The clinic director, Zoe, hurries to greet us, her intelligent eyes weary from managing the under-supplied facility. "Thank you for coming, all of you," she says earnestly. "Your blood donations are truly a lifeline for our patients." Though initially wary of our kind, Zoe has proven an advocate for bridging the divide between humans and Evols.

Inside the bustling clinic, nurses stand ready to draw blood at sterile stations, the chemical disinfectant unable to mask the sickness in the air. I sit beside Lily on cracking vinyl seats. It took time to bridge the gap between our kinds, but we're finally giving blood willingly.

As the needle pierces my skin, I'm thankful we've reached this point. River meets my eyes with purpose. We can't erase past horrors, but perhaps this act of compassion plants the first seeds of peace.

Afterward, we follow Zoe outside, where children flock around us, marveling. One boy around twelve timidly touches the tips of my feathers. I let him, smiling as his eyes widen. A young girl nearby stumbles, and I catch her, steadying her. She gazes up in awe. "You saved me."

I smooth back her hair. "We're here to help. That's what we do."

We say our goodbyes to the staff and prepare to leave.

"Wait," someone calls.

I turn with River, and a young woman who looks like twenty-three going on fifty approaches. The tired-eyed mother shifts a raggedy baby on her hip and clasps my hands, tearful. A rush of her hardships with her sick child goes through me. "You saved my boy," she says tearfully. "Your blood donation gave him life. Thank you."

Overwhelmed, I offer a comforting smile. As we turn to leave, the woman calls out, "Hold on." I pause.

"Maybe you're not so different after all. I won't forget what you've done."

I nod, surprised by her words. Her gratitude may be the first step toward healing between our kinds. As I look ahead, I envision a day when our people will extend hands of help— delivering food, medicine, and compassion. I know the doubts in their eyes all too well. Yet, deep down, I believe that despite our shared scars, we'll find a way to see and respect each other.

Today was the first fragile step toward reconciliation. It's enough.

As we fly home, I think of the children's awe and curiosity, a fragile chance for change.

Just last week, the schoolhouse welcomed two human children into class alongside the Evol students as part of an amicable experiment. The human children initially hesitated, casting shy glances at their winged classmates. But they chatted and laughed together by the end of the day's lessons. I caught a glimpse of them bounding through a hopscotch grid, laughing together as if their differences had never existed.

Perhaps such joyful connections will eventually outshine the painful legacy haunting us all. River and I will strive to teach our children compassion. We must believe humanity's goodness persists if given a chance to take root.

Epilogue

River

Five years later

"Daddy, look!" Griffin shouts, his tiny face alight with excitement. My four-year-old son leaps from the rocks, his downy wings outstretched. He manages a shaky but determined glide before landing unsteadily on the grass below. Peals of laughter follow.

I grin and ruffle his black hair. "Atta boy, you're getting there." His delight is infectious. Delene welcomes us back, hand on her pregnant belly. I kiss her and rest my hand over hers, eager to welcome our baby girl.

Down in the valley, life buzzes in Evol Hollow, the streets paved and a few horse-drawn carts clicking along the road. Lily and Adam's rambunctious twin girls, Aspen and Aria, play an energetic game of mid-air tag with the other Evol children. Curly red hair flying, Aspen waves eagerly as she zooms closer, always delighted to see her favorite aunt and uncle. Her twin Aria, more reserved but with a mischievous glitter in her eyes, gives us a quick smile before diving back into the high-flying fun.

"Daddy, let's go higher," Griffin begs.

I lift him onto my shoulders, and we soar together, his laughter echoing in my ears. The bright sky spreads vastly.

It's been seven years since we Evols claimed our place in this world, founding the hidden sanctuary of Evol Hollow in the valley. Though prejudice and fear still linger in human cities, we've lit up our little corner of the world.

Our community has grown strong, shielded by the mountains that once gave me solitary refuge. We learned healing takes a collective effort. My family and village are everything.

"Go faster," Griffin giggles.

I grin back at my wife and soar higher, obeying Griffin's command. When we were persecuted and running for our lives, I never dreamed a peaceful future was possible. But destiny surprised us, leading us to our hidden valley haven where we built trust between former enemies. We haven't erased the prejudices yet, but we'll overcome them one generation at a time.

On Griffin's eleventh birthday, laughter floats over the wind. I watch as Griffin patiently guides his younger sister, Seraphine, in gliding.

Aspen and Aria show off their mid-air stunts not far from them, drawing elated shrieks from my niece. Porter married Amanda, a newcomer to Evol Village, several years back, and he's never been happier.

Approaching Delene, I wrap my arms around her. With Delene nestled against me, warmth and gratitude flood my being. Nearby, our children play barefoot, their innocence untouched by the cruel world. Gazing at their joy, I know our struggles were worth it. We bled and battled to make this dream a reality.

Fourteen years after founding Evol Hollow, Delene and I walk through the valley hand-in-hand, taking in the sights.

At the village marketplace, Evol vendors and human customers now engage in friendly conversation, exchanging goods and medical remedies with genuine camaraderie. As an Evol healer, Delene has been instrumental in building trust between our kinds. Her compassion sets an example, overcoming lingering wariness.

There's still a long road ahead, and not everywhere outside our community is as accepting as we've become. Still, as I watch children — Evol and human — playing tag in the schoolyard, their laughter blending seamlessly, a surge of hope fills my heart.

More than twenty years have passed since we started our family, and triumphant cheers ring through the air as we watch Griffin marry his childhood sweetheart, Olivia.

Beside me, Delene cheers the loudest, and I join in, thrill coursing through me. Through misty eyes filled with pride, I watch our son. His wings catch the light as he turns to the crowd with his new bride, reflecting strength and confidence, propelling him into a future that seems limitless with promise.

Silver strands now weave through my hair, but as I greet Delene and step into our empty nester cabin, I can't help the mischievous sparkle in my eyes. Our love has only grown over time, a love we share with our ever-expanding family.

As elders, we lead the council and nurture the sapling of peace. There's more work ahead, but we walk together and find the answers in each other.

I once thought happiness was unattainable. But Delene and this family gave me purpose.

Now, in our sunset years, Delene and I recline in rocking chairs on our porch, watching our great-grandchildren play. Their laughter and unfettered joy are blessings. I lace my weathered fingers through Delene's, marveling at our long journey together. I see the same vibrant spirit I fell for all those years ago in her smiling eyes.

"We did good," I say, my voice thick with emotion.

Delene squeezes my hand, joy shining in her eyes. "We did."

I lean over and kiss her softly, infinitely grateful for a life lived to its fullest. Our ambitions took root and blossomed despite the ruins. And the seeds we planted will continue spreading light for generations to come.

It took me a while to figure this out, but love isn't a vulnerability. It's the most powerful force there is.

The End

OUR STREET
BOOKS

JUVENILE FICTION, NON-FICTION, PARENTING

Our Street Books are for children of all ages, delivering a potent
mix of fantastic, rip-roaring adventure and fantasy stories to
excite the imagination; spiritual fiction to help the mind and the
heart; humorous stories to make the funny bone grow;
historical tales to evolve interest; and all manner of subjects that
stretch imagination, grab attention, inform, inspire and keep
the pages turning. Our subjects include Non-fiction and Fiction,
Fantasy and Science Fiction, Religious, Spiritual, Historical,
Adventure, Social Issues, Humour, Folk Tales and more.
If you have enjoyed this book, why not tell other readers by
posting a review on your preferred book site.

Magnificent Me, Magnificent You – The Grand Canyon
Dawattie Basdeo, Angela Cutler
A treasure-filled story of discovery with a range of
inspiring fun exercises, activities, songs and games
for children aged 6 to 11.
Paperback: 978-1-78279-819-4

Q is for Question
An ABC of Philosophy
Tiffany Poirier
An illustrated non-fiction philosophy book to help
children aged 8 to 11 discover, debate and articulate
thought-provoking, open-ended questions about
existence, free will and happiness.
Hardcover: 978-1-84694-183-2

Relax Kids: How to be Happy
52 positive activities for children
Marneta Viegas
Fun activities to bring the family together.
Paperback: 978-1-78279-162-1

Rise of the Shadow Stealers
The Firebird Chronicles
Daniel Ingram-Brown
Memories are going missing. Can Fletcher and
Scoop unearth their own lost history and save the
Storyteller's treasure from the shadows?
Paperback: 978-1-78099-694-3 ebook: 978-1-78099-693-6

Readers of ebooks can buy or view any of these bestsellers by clicking on the live link in the title. Most titles are published in paperback and as an ebook. Paperbacks are available in traditional bookshops. Both print and ebook formats are available online.

Find more titles and sign up to our readers' newsletter at www.collectiveinkbooks.com/children-and-young-adult

Printed and bound by CPI Group (UK) Ltd, Croydon, CR0 4YY

20/01/2025

01823143-0004